Gripping, Fast-Paced, I Didn't Want It To End! A _Must_ Read! – Wendy Barker's Book Review (Seattle, WA) "*...A page-turner from start to finish, the story is fast-paced, filled with intrigue and action. I loved the ending, which keeps readers on the tips of their toes!*"

Happy to Recommend! – Molly Martin, Midwest Book Review (Oregon, WI)
"*...Chasing Diana is a fast-paced thriller sure to grab reader interest from the outset and hold it fast... Characters are colorful, varied and nicely detailed. Settings are fully developed, dialogue is gritty and hard hitting, the storyline is compelling. Danger, intrigue and deceit abound on the pages of this spell-binding work... filled with excitement, wit and gripping situations.*"

This Would Make A Great Movie! Fabulous! – Jodi Dorn (Alberta, Canada)
"*This book is the whole package: smart, entertaining and respectful. Once I started reading, I missed lunch and a nap just to finish it! The passion and fabulous energy behind the words are palpable. Thank you, Robin and Jack Firestone, for sharing your story with the world!*"

Written Brilliantly! – Rhonda Swan (San Diego, CA)
"*...Chasing Diana is written brilliantly, as each event played out vividly in my mind. I read the story in two hours... I couldn't put it down.*"

Breathless! – Verified Amazon Purchase, 5 stars – James Napoleon (CT)
"*To read the Firestones' raw-edged inspired-by-the-truth story is like being shot out of a cannon. You will be breathless and bruised, reliving this tragedy of a generation so close and so personal, as the Firestones embark on a 1990s vacation, hijacked by volatile forces out of control. Keep an open mind and stay with the churn of events, though it will at times break your heart. The Goodrich family survives a media feeding frenzy and the bizarre designs of some very desperate players. A truly original take on an event that will haunt us all for decades.*"

Reminiscent of Oliver Stone's JFK – Justin Paprocki, "The Island Packet," book reviewer (Hilton Head Island, SC)
"*Chasing Diana is reminiscent of Oliver Stone's 'JFK' which took the Kennedy assassination and added intrigue and conspiracy theory into a narrative telling of a lawyer trying to solve the president's death. Chasing Diana spins murderous paparazzi and crooked cops into its tale.*"

CHASING DIANA
Perception vs. Reality

Inspired by Our True Story

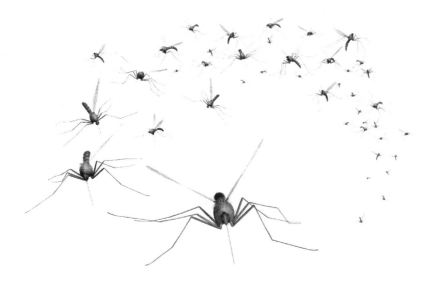

Written by American Eyewitnesses

Jack Firestone & Robin Firestone

SPECIAL EDITION

Includes "Tunnel Vision" by Jack Firestone
NEWLY FORMATTED AND REVISED 2017

This "screenplay novel" is historical fiction.

The central event of Princess Diana's death is factual, as are the names Dodi Al Fayed, Trevor Rees-Jones and Henri Paul. All other characters, names, places, dates and incidents are the products of the authors' imaginations, or are used fictitiously.

Table of Contents

Cast of Major Characters

Rhonda Goodrich — wife, mother, former actress
James Goodrich — husband, father, actor
Ben Goodrich — their crime-busting son
David Goodrich — James's brother, talent agent
Suzy Q — David's receptionist, his girlfriend

Jessica — wife, mother, irksome neighbor
Norman — husband, father, annoying neighbor
Chloe — their sweet daughter, Ben's close friend
Scott — their bothersome son

Monsieur Laurent — husband, father, former disgraced French police officer
Monique — wife, mother, mysterious espionage undercover spy
Jacques — their second eldest son, paparazzo
Rémy — their youngest son, reckless taxi driver
Pierre — their oldest son, limousine driver

Gerard Barbette — Brigade Criminelle Capitaine de Police
Interpreter — Brigade Criminelle employee
Inspecteur Marie Tiessart — Brigade Criminelle police officer

Ken Jarrett — CNN Paris bigshot
Richard Zimbalist — CNN Paris employee, bodyguard
Bob Feldman — CNN Paris senior producer
Walter Rodgers — CNN Paris senior reporter
Mindy Stevens — CNN Washington, D.C. segment producer
Judy Lyons — CNN New York City segment producer
Andrew Gates — *Time* magazine reporter

Concierge — Hôtel Vérité employee
Desk Clerk — Ritz Hotel employee

Interpol Agent — Paris division
Officer Le Baron — Paris division

Englishman With Derby — wealthy rogue

Steve Bernhardt — former actor, celebrity TV news host, movie producer
Photo Shop Employee — teenage entrepreneur
Jeff Smith — TV news producer

Bruno — restaurateur

Princess Diana
Dodi Al Fayed
Henri Paul
Trevor Rees-Jones

PRINCE HARRY, APRIL 2017

"I can safely say that losing my mum at the age of 12, and therefore shutting down all of my emotions for the last 20 years, has had quite a serious effect on not only my personal life but my work as well... my way of dealing with it was sticking my head in the sand, refusing to ever think about my mum, because why would that help?"

———

PRINCE WILLIAM, APRIL 2017

"The shock is the biggest thing, and I still feel it 20 years later about my mother. People think shock can't last that long, but it does. It's such an unbelievably big moment in your life and it never leaves you, you just learn to deal with it."

"History is stranger than fiction."

— Jack Firestone

". . . So nice to have known you,
although we've not met."

— Robin Firestone

In loving memory of our Moms, Betty & Carole

Author's Notes
Introduction by Robin Firestone

I STILL WONDER HOW THIS all even came to be. And I wonder "Why?" After all these years, I find myself searching for answers; searching for the truth. I often wonder if I will ever truly understand the meaning of life itself, and the unresolved circumstances of which we find ourselves in the midst. I believe I will, but if not in *this* lifetime, then certainly the next.

As a child I was very inquisitive and curious, constantly asking questions, certainly always asking "Why?" Most of the time I was satisfied with the answers provided, but not always. At times, my questions were answered with just a single word, a Yiddish word: "bashert" [pronounced *beh-sheert*]. It means "predestined or predetermined, fated, meant to be." In other words, "everything happens for a reason; there are no accidents."

Just weeks after turning 12-years-old, my life as a happy-go-lucky carefree child would never be the same. The date was July 24th, 1968: I remember it as though it was yesterday; the very moment that my larger-than-life, six-foot three-inch tall father – my hero! – uttered the most dreadful words that I had ever heard in my life. The words that he spoke tore away at my heart.

He had asked my grandmother to bring me and my older sister into a bedroom, and then told us to sit down. His huge dark brown eyes filled with tears, and, in as gentle a voice as he could muster, he spoke four words, "Mommy died last night." All I could hear was curdling screams, "No, No, No!!!..." I didn't realize it was me and my sister who were doing all the screaming.

"Mommy died last night," he had said, gently.

Even though more than forty years have passed as I write this, I still crumble like a child and break down in tears when I think back on that moment. The pain and loss of my mother will forever live inside of me.

I recall asking my father, "*Why* did mommy die?" I didn't understand. I realized that he didn't understand, either. "Why did

God take mommy away from us? How can we grow up without a mother?" Our younger sister had just turned 3-years-old, and my mom was *barely* more than a child herself when she passed away, having lost her life to cancer at just 33-years-old. I was in a state of shock and disbelief; I was numb and confused. My grief-stricken dad cradled his head in his hands; his head shook and he broke down. He held us so close and tight, with those baseball-mitt-sized hands of his, and he whispered "Everything will be alright." He let us know how much mommy loved us, as did he.

"Everything will be alright," he had said.

While I couldn't possibly understand at that time why God would take a mother away from her three young daughters, all I could tell myself was that God must have had a reason. It must have been bashert.

But my life lessons were far from over: Memorial Day, 1981, just two weeks after we had celebrated my 25th birthday, dad and I were in our house at midday as he suffered a massive heart attack. The emergency medical team who arrived lifted my father from his bed to the stretcher, and as they began to wheel him away into the ambulance waiting outside, he and I locked eyes. I'll never forget that. Neither of us said a word to the other, but we both knew it would be the very last time we'd see each other. It was a silent goodbye, but I never had a chance to actually *say* "goodbye"... to tell him how much I loved him. But I know he knows.

My dad passed away en route to the hospital at the young age of 49.

Now, I could have spent my life as a victim of tragedy, but I decided to choose to believe that there was yet another absolute lesson for me to learn. There *is* a reason for everything, and to get at the answers, one must dig deep into their soul.

More life lessons: In early 1986, some eight months after the birth of Jack's and my son, Brandon, when the oncologist told me I had just a 25% chance of surviving my recent diagnosis of cancer, I declared, "I will *not* die. I will *not* leave my son without his mother. I *will* be a part of his life and watch him grow up!" I beat the cancer, yet I often wonder why some people are meant to live long lives and others are meant to die young. The answer is simple; it is bashert.

So why was Princess Diana's life to end so tragically at just 36-years-old? And what placed *us* in the Alma Tunnel just moments after the deadly crash that took three lives in the wee hours of that morning? Why was *our* ordinary American family destined to become entangled in such a catastrophe? *Why?* Because it was our destiny.

This tragedy affected hundreds of millions of people from around the world, but for me, [and I'm sure for many, many others], it affected me on a very personal level. Perhaps it was because I was there, on site in the Alma Tunnel, and the shocking way in which I heard the words that it was Princess Diana who had died in that car crash, that the sudden, unexpected losses of my beautiful young mom and loving dad resurfaced.

I could feel the pain of her two young boys as Prince Charles broke the news of the death of their beloved mum to them. I shared their tender tears. I was overwhelmed emotionally and my entire being was in a state of transcendence.

I still have nightmares of what we witnessed in Paris. Why? Again, over and over again, I ask myself "Why?" Why were *we* in the middle of it all? I believe, with every fiber of my soul, that it was bashert. We were supposed to be there, just as our hotel was only steps away from the Ritz. Things in life happen for a reason, and I know that the events we were witness to were highly relevant; it would be mere indifference and morally unconscionable to write it off as coincidence. Yes, we were supposed to be there for a reason. It was bashert!

Our son Brandon, who was then 12-years-old – about the same age as Prince Harry was in 1997 – asked me the exact question I asked of my dad many years earlier, "How are they going to grow up without their mother?" And the memories came flooding back to me yet again.

I was numb, knowing all too well, first-hand, what those two young princes would miss without their mother to guide them in their lives. They'd go through life with a large piece of their soul missing. No mother to kiss them goodnight, to tell them that she loved them, to tell them that everything will be alright; no mother to watch them grow up, get married, and have children. There is no replacing the unconditional love of a mother!

So it was many years before I would agree to write this book with Jack. I buried my personal pain and feelings for so long, because I knew it would have an enormous effect on me and my family, as well as the Investigations. I can also admit now that I was honestly afraid, and had every reason to be! But I've come to realize that living one's life in a state of fear is not living at all.

Our lives were turned inside out and upside down. Imagine having the courage to go to the French police as witnesses to an event that had a huge impact on a family – a royal family, at that – as well as on England, on France, and on the entire planet, and then being told, "We have enough witnesses!" Imagine doing your civic duty, and knowing that the "investigations" that had subsequently taken place in the years that followed, were shams. Imagine your deposition being taken – only because CNN Paris had told the head of the initial French investigation in early September, 1997, that CNN would air an exposé on TV that night if the Firestones' were not deposed – and then having that same deposition "Missing In Action" for over ten years! And imagine hearing, as the years went by, over and over again, from both the French *and* British governments, that *all witnesses were called back to testify* during the first two Inquests. Yet we, as deposed witnesses from the outset – who went on *record* in September, 1997 – were *not* called back! "*Why?*"

Now imagine getting a telephone call from the office of the Chief Coroner, Lord Justice Scott Baker in London, to personally appear, and *finally* give testimony in the "*Third and Final Inquest.*" Imagine, in early December, 2007, over ten years after Diana's death, arriving in the courtroom of the Royal Courts of Justice in London, ready, willing and able to give never-before-heard eyewitness testimony. Imagine the bickering barristers, arguing back and forth, as to the reason why, when they had put Jack on the stand, that his line of questioning was filled with antagonism from Lord Justice Scott Baker, almost from the start! The barristers representing the court treated Jack with the same contempt. Jack wasn't on trial, yet he was treated that way! He was an eyewitness, for goodness' sake! Imagine when I heard the words straight out of Lord Justice Scott Baker's mouth, after Jack's forty-five minute testimony, that "they" were running over schedule, that he was hungry and wanted to break for lunch, and that there would be no need to hear further testimony from eyewitness Robin Firestone! Imagine the flurry in the courtroom when the barristers for Mohamed Al Fayed, on behalf of his late son Dodi, reminded Lord Justice Scott Baker why he called *us* – to fly both Jack *and me* from New York to London – to give *live* testimony! Jack and I even paid our own way for the airfare and the hotel! Truth, justice and liberty for all...? I think not. [P.S. The "good Lord" Baker finally – under pressure from Al Fayed's barristers – agreed to let me take the witness stand as a cursory gesture. In order to placate those barristers, I was questioned for an obligatory, yet mere, five minutes, after which I was released as a witness... but not before I gave Lord Justice Baker a little piece of my mind!]

For well over ten years, Jack and I felt like we were characters in a conspiracy-laden, international murder mystery movie. The initial version of our book, never published under legal advice, was written as 100% non-fiction. We were immediately advised to re-write the book and, for our protection, to change the names and some of the facts. Jack and I thought about this for quite some time, and mutually decided that it would, in fact, make the most sense to re-write the book in the form of a theatrical motion picture screenplay, so as to give you, the reader, a vicarious sense of what we experienced – "you are there" – so *Chasing Diana* became historical fiction, which is *inspired* by our true story.

You will read, first-hand, that *Chasing Diana* is not just another book about the tragic death of a royal princess. It's not really about that at all, except on the surface. Instead, this is a story of how a family almost got torn apart in its midst, as a result of witnessing what they did. This book is, at the same time, also about the calamity of errors in the initial investigations themselves. This book is about weaving reality with fantasy to make a statement, as well as for the sake of the innocent people involved. This book is about getting out of one's comfort zone and reading in-between the lines. This book is about loss and vulnerability. This book is about love, honor and justice. This book is about closure: it's about standing up for yourself, regardless of who looks to stand in your way. This book was also written in order to keep the many unanswered questions about the death of Princess Diana and Dodi Al Fayed alive, so we can always be reminded that we want *truthful* answers... not convenient answers! *Chasing Diana: Inspired by Our True Story* was written for many reasons. And it was written because it was bashert.

Robin Firestone
Hilton Head Island, SC
February 23, 2012

Author's Notes
Introduction by Jack Firestone

DURING THE SUMMER OF '97, Robin, our son Brandon and I witnessed a horrific, yet historic, devastating international incident that would forever change my view of just how precarious the narrow line that separates life from death is.

At roughly half-past midnight on Sunday, August 31st, inside the Pont de l' Alma Tunnel in Paris, we three witnessed the immediate aftermath of the car crash that snuffed out the flame of life which had belonged to Princess Diana. We had arrived in Paris less than a dozen hours before, as part of the itinerary which Robin had so diligently put together for our family vacation. Robin was serious about us three seeing as many sites as time permitted, and so far, that consisted of an incredible one week's stay in London, followed by what was *supposed* to be a vacation of three days and three nights in Paris. But on that late August night, the vacation came to a complete and abrupt halt; the holiday was over, and the work was about to begin. This would be the beginning of a brand new, multi-layered chapter in our lives, the memories of which will remain with us forever.

That night, after hours of sightseeing, I was exhausted and looking forward to getting back to our hotel; the hour was late, but we had enjoyed ourselves so much on that first night – drinking in all the beauty which Paris had to offer – that we were barely aware of the time. Robin and Brandon could hardly wait for more sightseeing fun the next day, but, truth be told, *I* would have been just fine, thank you, to slow down the sightseeing pace for the Paris portion of our trip. [Be careful what you ask for, 'cause you just might get it.]

But slowing down the sightseeing pace wasn't what Robin had planned from the outset, as she was on a mission: having so deftly coordinated the countless tours on which we went in England during the previous week – by weeks' end, I felt like an honorary Brit! – I knew she had done the same thing for Paris, so I just, in effect, went along for the ride. But little did I know that the two galaxies of Great

Britain and France were about to collide, as we found ourselves inextricably intertwined within the confines of an international event of catastrophic proportions.

As human beings, we live our lives from moment to moment, never really knowing what may await us just around the corner. Often, "the best laid plans" go astray, as I have found out several times in my life. One cannot fight what is either meant, or not meant, to be. Everything happens for a reason; sometimes the reason becomes immediately evident, and other times it can take days, months – even years – for the "reason" to become perfectly clear.

Okay, let's get back to how we were in the wrong (or right) place at the right (or wrong) time. After a scenic one hour sightseeing tour on the River Seine, in order to get back to our hotel, we hailed a taxi and the three of us climbed into the rear seat of the cab. [You know, I had read or heard somewhere that French drivers, in the main, have this reputation of possessing driving habits which are highly reckless, as regards obeying the posted speed limits. Was this true? I was about to find out, first-hand.] Suffice it to say that our cabbie was of that speed-demon variety, and his driving skills literally scared the hell out of us as he zipped along the mostly empty avenue at incredibly high kilometers per hour. In a brief moment of time, we became helpless American captives sitting in the rear seat of a taxi, silently praying. The silence was brief, as it took place in between the driver's inane rantings and our pleas for him to keep his eyes on the road. For whatever reason, still unknown to me – I hope it wasn't just because we were an *American* family – and despite the numerous shouts I made for our cabbie to slow down before he got us all killed in a car crash, this particular French driver, with every one of our pleas, felt "egged on," it seemed, and would then, belligerently, drive even faster. And there was nothing any of us could do about it.

Luckily – eventually – there was a lot of traffic that I saw approaching up ahead; traffic never looked so good to me in my life. But our cabbie was now travelling so fast that he was unable to detour away from it; he had no choice but to step on the brakes and immediately start to slow down the cab and, in the process, we become a part of the barrage of cars which would soon enter the now infamous Alma Tunnel underpass, heading eastward, as was the direction in which we were headed.

And so we entered the underpass, entrenched in a stop-and-go traffic jam. Up ahead, just around the slight curve of the Tunnel, I expected that we would soon find out the cause of the congestion, as I had seen blue flashing lights reflected off the Tunnel walls up ahead. As we came upon those lights, we saw there had been a horrendous car crash, and as we finally arrived on scene, our madman driver put the taxi in 'Park.' One couldn't help take in what was happening at the crash site: there was a band of pursuing photographers, closing in on the prey for the final kill, smothering the carnage as they advanced on foot with their hand-held machines of death [that is to say, their flash cameras], offering no aid to the victims, whomever they might be, in the wreckage. If this was forensic police work, as I initially thought, then I suppose one could say that they were just doing their jobs. But it was obvious, really, from the pent up fervor at the crash site that this was not police science work at all, but rather, something was going on here that reeked of being even *worse* than unscrupulous human behavior. ¡Qué lástima!

I later put two and two together, and realized that these very well could have been some of the people who were hovering at the rear of the Ritz Hotel whom we had seen earlier in the day, about which I'll discuss more in a moment: the paparazzi. And it was clear to me, upon reflection, that they had an agenda, which was to take as many photos as possible of the doomed passengers in that vehicle of death. One thing was for certain: the paparazzi knew that their photos would be worth a king's ransom. *They* knew who they were photographing; one could just tell. One might even go further and say that the paparazzi had picked the bones clean, so to speak, like a pack of hovering vultures. And for a minute or so, our family had a bird's-eye view of this barbarous behavior. As tourists in a foreign country, with no exact idea of what was unfolding in front of our eyes, all we could do was to be what we were: spectators. [If I've not yet made it clear, by the way, none of us sitting in the rear seat of the taxi had any idea whatsoever that one of the victims inside that crashed car was Princess Diana – I'm not so certain of our driver's knowledge, however – but *we* didn't find out who was killed in the crash until after we ate breakfast later that morning.]

Interestingly enough, only ten hours prior to that ill-fated car crash, at roughly the same time of day, on Saturday afternoon, August 30th, our family, and Diana & Dodi, independently of one another, all arrived in Paris simultaneously, the former by Chunnel train and the latter by private plane. We even stayed at a hotel whose front entrance was some two hundred feet or so diagonally across the street from the rear exit to the now infamous revolving doors of the Ritz Hotel; and as it happened, when we exited our hotel and were on the street at about 5:30 P.M. that first afternoon in Paris, getting ready to start our sightseeing adventures, we were watching the antics of a large group of photographers who were congregating in front of those revolving doors at the rear of the Ritz; Brandon and I thought maybe they were filming a movie, so, being an actor, we went to check it out. Nope, no movie; in retrospect, it was just a lot of stalking. Of course, I had no idea that these people could have been part of the group of animals who would, in the hours to come, be responsible for the death of a former royal princess and her boyfriend.

Again, all of this happened during our first evening in Paris. But I believe that all things that happen, happen for a reason, as Robin has written about in regard to bashert. Was the reason we were on site so that we could tell the tale of the ineptness of the initial French investigations into Diana's and Dodi's deaths at some future Inquest? Was the reason so that we could be witnesses to Diana's death, and therefore, even though she and Dodi have passed on, we could continue to keep their story alive until justice hopefully prevails one day? Or was it some other reason that has yet to show itself, even as you read this.

By the way, the ultimate spark which ignited our decision to write *Chasing Diana: Inspired by Our True Story* came about as a result of an article Robin had first read in the October, 2004 edition of *Vanity Fair* magazine. Robin left the article open on my side of the bed for me; she basically said, "Jack, you won't believe this; read it!" I did, and she was right. I had read how Scotland Yard had reopened the initial French judicial investigation into Diana's death, which had lasted some 18 months [having concluded in 1999.] In brief, the *Vanity Fair* piece went on to say that the French investigation, for a number of reasons, was botched. Based on what we knew, we couldn't have agreed more. *That* was my impetus for setting this story down in print. I had kept a journal when we arrived home in early September, 1997, which provided me with a great many of the details and musings of which you're about to read. I got to work on the first draft, but realized that I could not write this book alone. I required Robin's assistance and collaboration, and she was, for a couple of years, highly reticent. She told me she was scared; she told me she was concerned about what others might think. As Robin explained in the previous section, she eventually got over those fears, particularly by utilizing many of the precepts of personal transformation and self improvement techniques. [If you've never read *The Traveler's Gift* by Andy Andrews, we highly recommend it; you'll then have a full understanding of how Robin got over her plight as to whether or not to co-author this book with me.]

But I digress. What really got my blood boiling was the fact that, again, in that *Vanity Fair* article, it went on to say that every witness had been called back to testify, either in France or in the U.K. Well, we weren't. You know, it's not as if we were *strangers* to this case. In other words, we had gone on record numerous times over the intervening years, having been interviewed by CNN, both in Paris and in the USA, having been quoted in subsequent newspaper articles and interviewed by several network TV programs. So my thinking was, if *we* were never called back for either the initial French Investigation or the 2004 British Inquest, then one could infer that there were lots of other witnesses who were never called back, either. Had they called us back, this book would never even have been written! Was I up to the challenge to make sure that I could let the world know that there were egregious mistakes in what the public was being told? Yes, but only if Robin chose to get out of her comfort zone and collaborate with me, and that was a decision only Robin could make for herself.

With each passing year, I would reflect on the fact that there were, perhaps, dark, conspiratorial forces at play that took place that night in late August '97. Maybe we weren't called back either of those two times, I surmised, because Robin and I were unknown quantities – loose cannons, if you will – in terms of what we might say. In other words, maybe the "powers that be" decided that the Firestones' testimony, which, if given live to the courts, might be akin to a jigsaw puzzle piece. Our "puzzle piece" could never be a part of that already completed picture which appears on the top of the jigsaw puzzle box, if all of the puzzle pieces had been prefabricated ahead of time, made to interlock. Perhaps they didn't want to hear any testimony which might shed additional light on the possibility that Diana's and Dodi's deaths were premeditated.

In any event, the theme of *Chasing Diana: Inspired by Our True Story* is as relevant today as it was in 1997, perhaps even *more* so today: fame [unwitting or not], combined with the media spotlight, can be very hazardous to your health. Our fictional counterparts – Rhonda and James Goodrich – experience the heady highs and the abysmal lows that unwitting notoriety brings with it. As my alter ego James would probably say, "Be careful what you wish for 'cause you just might get it. And then, there's the piper to pay."

So we present to you, dear reader, a behind-the-scenes look, *inspired* by our true story, of what we had experienced during those three days and three nights in Paris, and beyond. I suggest that, in a number of cases, you read *between* the lines for the bigger truths.

As I see it, the human condition is basically a darkly-humored three-act play, a frail drama of people making comedic errors... or is it a frail comedy of people making dramatic missteps? Maybe it's both, at different times.

Jack Firestone
Hilton Head Island, SC
February 23, 2012

Screenplay Jargon

*Here are some useful definitions of terms used
in the "Chasing Diana" screenplay*

Act - used in screenwriting and playwriting, the model that divides a fictional narrative into three parts (acts), often called the Setup, the Confrontation and the Resolution

Action - the moving pictures we see on screen. Also, the direction given by a director indicating that filming begins

Character - any personified entity appearing in a play or movie. The first time the character appears, his or her name is in upper case

Character arc - the emotional progress of the characters during their story

Character name - when any character speaks, his or her name appears on the line preceding the dialogue. In screenplays, the name is tabbed to a location that is roughly in the center of the line

CONT'D - dialogue spoken by the same character that continues uninterrupted

Establishing Shot - a cinematic shot that establishes a certain location or area

EXT. - the scene takes place outside

FLASHBACK - a scene from the past that interrupts the action to explain motivation or reaction of a character to the immediate scene

INT. - the scene takes place indoors

O.C. - abbreviation for Off Camera, denoting that the speaker resides within the scene but is not seen by the camera

O.S. - abbreviation for Off Screen, denoting that the speaker is physically not present in the scene

TITLE OVER - text that appears onscreen denoting a key element of the movie, a change of location or date, or person involved in the making of the movie

Parenthetical - an inflection of speech or a character's physical movement

Scene - action taking place in one location and in a distinct time that moves the story to the next element of the story

Scene Heading - a short description of the location and time of day of a scene, also known as a "slugline." For example, INT. MUSEUM - LATER - DAY would denote that the action takes place inside a museum during daylight hours

Screenplay or **Script** - the blueprint or roadmap that outlines a movie story through visual descriptions, actions of characters, and their dialogue

SMASH CUT - a quick or sudden cut from one scene to another

V.O. - abbreviation for Voice Over, denoting that the speaker is narrating the onscreen action

courtesy of www.screenwriting.info

Crash Site Roadway Map
August 31, 1997

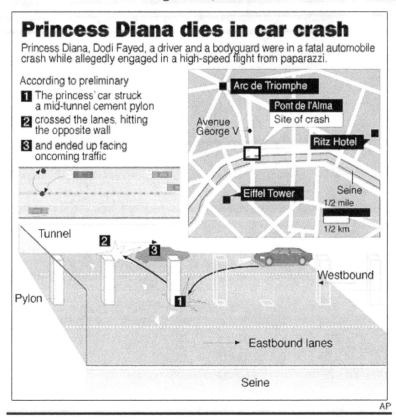

Princess Diana dies in car crash

Princess Diana, Dodi Fayed, a driver and a bodyguard were in a fatal automobile crash while allegedly engaged in a high-speed flight from paparazzi.

According to preliminary

1 The princess' car struck a mid-tunnel cement pylon

2 crossed the lanes, hitting the opposite wall

3 and ended up facing oncoming traffic

Arc de Triomphe

Pont de l'Alma
Site of crash

Avenue George V

Ritz Hotel

Eiffel Tower

Seine
1/2 mile
1/2 km

Tunnel

Pylon

Westbound

Eastbound lanes

Seine

AP

Inspired by Our True Story

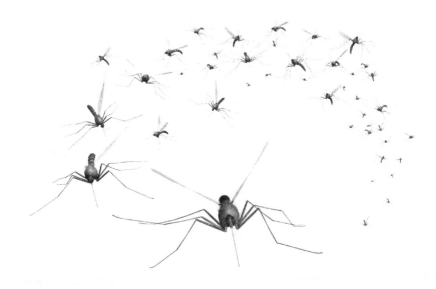

per·cep·tion
pərˈsepSH(ə)n/

noun

- a way of regarding, understanding, or interpreting something

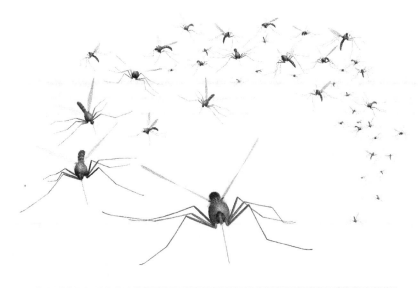

PRO-
LOGUE
August 1998

New York & Paris

FADE IN:

EXT. JFK AIRPORT - NIGHT

Clear skies, moonlit evening, busy airport.
Perfect night to fly. A Concorde jet comes in
for a landing.

TITLE OVER:

"...SO NICE TO HAVE KNOWN YOU, ALTHOUGH
WE'VE NOT MET."

-- RHONDA GOODRICH

RHONDA'S VOICE (V.O.)
So nice to have known you, although
we've not met.

TITLE OVER: AUG. 1998, JFK AIRPORT, NEW YORK

EXT. AIR FRANCE TERMINAL, JFK AIRPORT - NIGHT

Black Mercedes limo parks in front of
"Departures - Air France" terminal.

RHONDA GOODRICH, mid 30's, dressed to the
nines, emerges with designer handbag.

JAMES GOODRICH, late 30's, sharply dressed,
climbs out other door, joins wife, curbside.

AMERICAN LIMO DRIVER #1 unloads a ton of
designer luggage from trunk. SKY CAP approaches
with cart.

                    SKY CAP
          Evening, folks. Where ya headed?

Rhonda hands him plane tickets. He glances at
them, grins.

                    SKY CAP (CONT'D)
          You guys *movin'* to France?

                    RHONDA
          Nope, just a couple few nights.

                    SKY CAP
          I see that. Wait a second, *the*
          Rhonda Goodrich? Oh man, my wife
          loves you. You're doin' the Oprah
          show in Paris, right?

                    JAMES
          Wrong. Oprah's doin' our show.

Rhonda rolls her eyes. James gives him a
friendly wink.

INT. AIR FRANCE TICKET COUNTER - MINUTES LATER

A throng of PASSENGERS in terminal.

Sleazy ROGUE COP covertly watches Rhonda and
James.

                    TICKET AGENT
          We board at 11:50, First Class
          lounge is on Level Two. And break a
          leg with that interview, Mrs. G.

Rhonda and James smile, walk away, boarding
passes in hand.

PRESS PHOTOGRAPHERS appear, snapping photos.
Rogue Cop sneaks towards lounge.

You checked out the following items:

1. Chasing Diana : perception vs. reality : inspired by our true story
Barcode: 30210312947145
Due: 2/20/2020
2. Me & Lee : how I came to know, love and lose Lee Harvey Oswald
Barcode: 30210312932188
Due: 2/20/2020
3. Jacqueline Bouvier Kennedy Onassis : the untold story
Barcode: 30210312551004
Due: 2/20/2020

You saved $66.89
by borrowing from the library.

01-23-2020 4:28:59 pm

COMMUNITY LIBRARY
740-965-3901
www.yourcl.org

You checked out the following items:

1. Chasing Diana : perception vs. reality : inspired by our true story
Barcode: 30210312947145
Due: 2/20/2020

2. Me & Lee : how I came to know, love and lose Lee Harvey Oswald
Barcode: 30210312932188
Due: 2/20/2020

3. Jacqueline Bouvier Kennedy Onassis : the untold story
Barcode: 30210312551004
Due: 2/20/2020

01-23-2020 4:26:59 pm

INT. OUTSIDE GLASS DOOR, FIRST CLASS LOUNGE -
MOMENTS LATER

Rogue Cop, behind potted plant, speaks into
flip cell phone.

> ROGUE COP
> Great news, Lieutenant Barbette. No
> change in plans. They depart for
> Paris in one hour.

EXT. BRIGADE CRIMINELLE BUILDING, PARIS -
CONTINUOUS - DAWN

> TITLE OVER: BRIGADE CRIMINELLE BUILDING,
> PARIS

Lieutenant GERARD BARBETTE, late 40's,
unshaven, dishevelled, flip cell phone in hand,
walks briskly towards building.

> GERARD BARBETTE
> I have dreamed of this day, this...
> réunion. It is long overdue.

He disconnects the call, checks his gun,
sprints up the steps. GUARD #1 opens one of the
formidable doors.

> GERARD BARBETTE (CONT'D)
> Interpol. My office. Stat.

Guard #1 nods, salutes. Gerard Barbette walks
inside.

INT. FIRST CLASS LOUNGE - MINUTES LATER - NIGHT

Rhonda and James sit at a private table,
replete with hors d'oeuvres. French Gloved
BUTLER pours champagne.

                    RHONDA
          Two Perriers instead, please? So!
          Ready for the Ritz? James, I can't
          believe they're flying us in on the
          Concorde.

Butler pours Perrier. The Goodrichs clink their
flutes.

                    JAMES
          Reading my mind, babe. You know, I
          was wondering... think Oprah's
          gonna let us keep the miles?

                    RHONDA
          Don't ask her that, Jim.

                    JAMES
          Really? Hey, one sec.

James snaps his fingers at Butler.

                    JAMES (CONT'D)
          Garçon. Two Stolis, straight up?

Rhonda glares. James is all innocence.

                    JAMES (CONT'D)
          What? Daddio promoted me today. I'm
          the new head veep of Sub-prime
          Mortgages. *No credito? No problemo!*

FEMALE FAN, holding pen and book, approaches
Rhonda. Book has photo of Rhonda on its back
cover.

                    FEMALE FAN
          I loved your book and your movie
          was awesome. Would you mind?

                    RHONDA
          My pleasure. James?

                          8

James takes the book. He knows the drill. His pen is ready.

                    JAMES   RHONDA
          First name, darlin'?   (aside, to Butler)
                                    Cancel the booze.

                    FEMALE FAN
          Debi. One b one i.

Rhonda finds emery board in her purse. She starts to file.

                    JAMES
          "*To Debra,*" one b, one i. "*Fondly,
          etcetera etcetera.*" There ya go,
          Deb, bye now. Garçon? Those drinks?

Female Fan walks away.

                    JAMES (CONT'D)
          Hey darlin', have I told you lately
          how much I love bein' your book
          signin' bitch? Now where the fuck's
          that waiter at?

EXT. CONCORDE JET - 7 HOURS LATER - MORNING

          TITLE OVER: 7 HOURS LATER, DE GAULLE
          AIRPORT, PARIS

The Goodrichs are on the tarmac. PASSENGERS exit the jet's stairway. AIRLINE EXEC #1 approaches, flashes official ID.

                    AIRLINE EXEC #1
          Mr. and Mrs. James Goodrich?

James nods.

                    AIRLINE EXEC #1 (CONT'D)
          Important. Follow me, please.

Rhonda glares at James.

                    JAMES
          Hey, the producers promised me and
          I made it very clear. No press, no
          paparazzi. This is bullshit...
          damned if ya, and damned if ya.

EXT. AIRPORT TRAM - MINUTES LATER

Rhonda, James, Airline Exec #1, Passengers all
stand on moving tram. Rhonda is pissed. James
is silently fuming.

INT. AIRPORT MANAGER'S OFFICE - MINUTES LATER

Rhonda, James, Airline Exec #1 enter. AIRPORT
MANAGER, AIRLINE EXEC #2, INTERPOL AGENT
approach.

                    INTERPOL AGENT
          Passports, s'il vous plait. You are
          both under arrest. For fraud.

Rhonda and James look at each other, jaws
agape.

     MAIN TITLE UP: CHASING DIANA: INSPIRED BY
     OUR TRUE STORY

END OF PROLOGUE.

ACT ONE
August 1997

New York & London & Paris

INT. RECEPTION, GOODRICH TALENT AGENCY - 1 YEAR
AGO - DAY

TITLE OVER: AUG. 1997, 1 YEAR EARLIER, NEW
YORK

James bursts into office, large envelope falls
from his grip. He picks it up, and also selects
the July 1997 Vanity Fair from coffee table's
magazine stack. He staggers to a seat.

He dry swallows two blue pills.

Some ACTORS and ACTRESSES in the room try to
conceal smirks.

SUZY Q, early 20's, very attractive
receptionist, smiles kindly at him. She presses
intercom button.

                    SUZY Q
          David can see you now, James.

                    JAMES
               (slurry)
          Tell Señor Goodwrench I come in
          peace.

He stands, kisses her cheek. She reels at his
alcohol breath. He chugs from her water bottle,
gargles, and tosses the Vanity Fair back on top
of magazine stack.

It lands face up, revealing the cover photo:
Princess Diana.

                    JAMES (CONT'D)
          Ha ha, two points! Still got it.

DAVID'S OFFICE - MOMENTS LATER

James bursts through door, drops the large
envelope again.

DAVID GOODRICH, mid-30's, overweight, wears an
expensive suit and red bow tie... and white
powder under his nostrils.

They high five.

      JAMES   DAVID GOODRICH
  Davy boy!   Jimbo, my main man.

David snorts a hit of coke. He offers a hit to
James, who declines. No problemo. David snorts
it.

         JAMES
    Wipe it, man. Your nose.

       DAVID GOODRICH
    (sniffs the air)
  Jumpin' juniper, is it gin o'clock
  already? Okay, lemme see 'em.

James picks up envelope, takes out a few 8 x 10
black & white headshots of himself, selects
one.

        JAMES
    (hiccups)
  I love this one, it's--

David selects a different photo.

       DAVID GOODRICH
  No no no, *this* one's the money
  shot. Yeah, good, make me a hundred
  copies. Okay, brother man, I'm
  like... bursting at the seams here.

                    JAMES
          Pants *are* lookin' a tad snug there,
          Davy. Got me some Fen-Phen. Want?

                    DAVID GOODRICH
          Paramount called.

James is at rapt attention.

                    DAVID GOODRICH (CONT'D)
          Bruce saw your taped audition,
          absolutely loves you, his people
          love you, and you're booked for a
          live callback in L.A. next Friday.

                    JAMES
          Knew it! Now that's what I'm
          talkin' about, baby. Rhonda's gonna
          be thrilled. Beautiful job, bro.

David snorts two more hits, thumbs through
Variety.

                    DAVID GOODRICH
          Hey, it's what I do. And yes, she
          is a beautiful job. She ever think
          about, you know, gettin' back in
          the ol' saddle again? Ben's old
          enough now and--

                    JAMES
          It's got nothing to do with Ben.

James hiccups, takes coke vial, snorts a couple
hits.

                    JAMES (CONT'D)
          She's so fucking jealous of me.
          "The residuals on your Coke spot
          ain't cuttin' it" and... um, what
          were we sayin'?

David can't remember either. James snorts
another hit.

                  JAMES (CONT'D)
Oh yeah. Know any good divorce
lawyers, man?

James's cell phone RINGS. He looks at it, not
happy.

                  JAMES (CONT'D)
Oh fuck, it's Big Brother.
      (into phone)
Honey darlin', just talkin' about
you. Hey, guess who's got a live
callback in Friday next L.A.?
      (beat)
The Ruce Billis peeps wanna see me.
      (beat)
Earth to Rhonda. Houston, we have--

INT. SUPERMARKET AISLE - CONTINUOUS

BEN GOODRICH, 12, nice kid, wise beyond his
years, pushes a half-full shopping cart.

Rhonda stands next to a precariously piled
pyramid display of tuna cans. Cell phone to one
ear, she selects a couple of cans, puts them in
cart, reaches for more.

                RHONDA
All lit up again, Jim... we're
flying to England next Friday,
darling. Remember?

              JAMES'S VOICE (V.O.)
      (hiccups)
London. Right.

                RHONDA
Ben's only been talking about this
for months. How many drinks today?
      (beat)
Anyhow, I had luncheon with Daddio
and he's not a happy pappy. He's

pressing the pause button on el
trusto fundo. He wants you to come
work for his mortgage--

RHONDA (CONT'D)	JAMES'S VOICE (V.O.)
...company. It would be perfect. You can finally start making a salary and--	Would you stop with that mortgage shit? I don't wanna work for your father. Hello?

Pyramid display of tuna cans COLLAPSES
LOUDLY, spilling onto Rhonda. She falls to
floor, her cell phone goes flying.

Ben and STORE CLERK run to her side.

                    BEN
        Mom!

INT. DAVID'S OFFICE - CONTINUOUS

James hears the LOUD COLLAPSE.

                    JAMES
        Hello? You there?

Looks at cell phone, snaps it shut.

David looks at him a moment, then goes back to
thumbing through Variety. Something's up.

                    JAMES (CONT'D)
        Dropped call.
             (beat)
        You gotta change that callback.

                    DAVID GOODRICH
        Because...

                    JAMES
        End of summer family trip. Leaving
        next Friday for a week in England,
        then Paris. Ben's really been--

>   DAVID GOODRICH
> Jesus Christ, Jimmy, I work my ass
> off to... ah, the life of a kept
> man, I guess. Nice job if you can--

>   JAMES
> Hey! Kept man, your ass.

James storms towards door.

>   DAVID GOODRICH
> Just a joke, Jimbro. I can change
> the callback date, okay? No prob.

>   JAMES
> Listen good. I don't wanna hear you
> talkin' about Rhonda and show biz
> in the same sentence, ever. And
> she's not a "beautiful job,"
> asswife, she's my freaking wipe.
> Get it?

James stumbles back to David's desk, snatches
chosen photo.

>   JAMES (CONT'D)
> I'll leave the copies with Suzy Q.
> Now *she*... is a beautiful job.

James exits, SLAMS door shut. David is
unperturbed.

He waits a moment, opens a bottom drawer,
removes a stack of old 8 x 10 B&W headshots.
Photos of a much younger Rhonda, and printed on
bottom of each: "RHONDA MORELAND."

>   DAVID GOODRICH
> Yup. These are the money shots.

INT. OUTER HALLWAY - MOMENTS LATER

James is about to close "Goodrich Talent Agency" door, leans back into reception area. Blows kiss to Suzy Q. She grins.

> SUZY Q
> Sounds like that went well.

She blows kiss back. He winks, forces a smile, shuts door.

He takes a couple more pills, swigs from his flask. Leans back against wall, slides down, sits on floor. Total woe.

INT. SUPERMARKET AISLE - MOMENTS LATER

Rhonda, on the floor, removes tuna cans from her body. Gets back on her feet with Ben's help. A small CROWD gathers.

Store Clerk and STORE MANAGER pile tuna cans into her cart.

JESSICA, late 30's, buxom blonde, overly made-up, appears with "plain Jane" daughter CHLOE, 12 going on 16, wearer of funky glasses and hot-pink colored braces.

> CHLOE
> You okay, Mrs. G.?

> STORE MANAGER
> So sorry, ma'am. Groceries on us today, okay?

> BEN
> Actually, sir, they're on my mom.

Ben and Chloe high five.

> RHONDA
> Oh, I'm terrific, Chloe. I wear the albacore well, don'tcha think? Or maybe chunk light is more my style.

                    JESSICA
          Yes, I'd definitely say chunk. Oh,
          look at you, poor dear, you tore
          your blouse. And a Dress Barn
          original? That's gotta hurt.
                    (to Chloe)
          Let's go.

Jessica pulls her down the aisle. Chloe waves
goodbye.

                    JESSICA (CONT'D)
          People will do anything for
          attention. And stay away from that
          wiseguy kid. His parents are
          pathetic and the apple doesn't fall
          far, ya know?

                    CHLOE
          But I really like Ben, mom.

                    JESSICA
          Well, he wouldn't be my choice.

                    RHONDA
                    (under her breath)
          Beach blonde bimbo bitch.

Her cell phone RINGS. Ben answers it.

                    BEN
          Hope you like tuna casserole, dad.

Rhonda grabs phone.

                    RHONDA
          You better straighten up and fly
          right, mister. You're going for
          help as soon as we get back or it's
          over.

She flips the phone shut, begins to sob. Ben
hugs her.

EXT. HEATHROW AIRPORT, LONDON - DAYS LATER -
MORNING

A busy airport. British Airways jet comes in
for landing.

TITLE OVER: SAT., AUG. 23, 1997, HEATHROW
AIRPORT, LONDON

EXT. VARIOUS SITES, LONDON - MONTAGE - DAY /
NIGHT

Double-decker buses, big black taxis, red phone
booths, bobbies, Big Ben, the Tower of London,
the Thames River...

The Goodrichs sight-see, window shop, dine...

James takes photos with his 35mm flash camera
which he keeps in a belt-loop camera case.

EXT. STREET VIEW, HARRODS - DAYS LATER - DAY

The sign for Harrods Dept. Store is immediately
recognizable on the posh Kensington corner. On
the street below, Rhonda hurries James and Ben
towards the entrance.

INT. HARRODS - 1 HOUR LATER

Rhonda receives change for her purchase of a
Princess Diana Beanie Baby. James and Ben carry
packages.

EXT. HARRODS, ELEGANT EXIT DOOR - MINUTES LATER

DOORMAN, 80's, stoic, dressed as a royal
Beefeater in complete regalia, holds the door
open.

                    RHONDA
          Loving them duds!

Doorman says nothing, maintains his posture.

                    RHONDA (CONT'D)
          Okay, I gotta ask. Have you ever
          seen Princess Diana here?

                    DOORMAN
          Oh, all the time. Her best mate,
          Dodi? His father keeps an office on
          the top floor. A lovely lady that
          Diana is, a real People's Princess.
          I simply adore her!
               (in confidence)
          I can't say that about ol' what's-
          his-name, the, ugh, *Prince*.

                    RHONDA
          Any chance of us running into her,
          ya think?

                    DOORMAN
          Not bloody likely, I should say.
          Word has it she is vacationing on
          Dodi's private yacht, as we speak.

EXT. SMALL BOAT, MEDITERRANEAN SEA - MOMENTS
LATER - DAY

ROCK MUSIC wafts softly from an anchored
distant yacht.

JACQUES, mid 20's, tanned, mustached paparazzo,
sits in passenger chair.

He looks through eyepiece of his camera's long
telephoto lens, snapping photos of distant
yacht.

INTERCUT: Several snapshots of PRINCESS DIANA
and DODI AL FAYED lounging on yacht.

MONSIEUR LAURENT, mid 60's, unshaven,
pockmarked, prominent buck teeth, smokes a
cigarette, wears an old T-shirt, sits in the
captain's chair.

He wears a Paris police cap, backward, police
badge affixed. He glances portside.

> MONSIEUR LAURENT
> (in French)
> Yes, there's a small gold mine in
> those photos, Jacques, but I lined
> up the ultimate job. And here it
> comes.

He points.

A 65-foot Hatteras yacht races towards them,
full throttle. Its ENGINE ROARS as it slows
down, approaches their small boat. The engine
is cut. The SILENCE is deafening.

The Hatteras drifts twenty feet away, a SKIPPER
at its helm.

ENGLISHMAN WITH DERBY, 35, dressed in expensive
suit, cocky, stands on Hatteras's main deck.

> ENGLISHMAN WITH DERBY
> I trust that retirement is treating
> you well, "Officer" Laurent?

> MONSIEUR LAURENT
> No small talk. Where's my money?

Englishman tosses burlap satchel to Laurent's
boat. Laurent tries to catch it, but fumbles.
Jacques picks it up.

Laurent grabs it, rips it open, starts to count
the money.

ENGLISHMAN WITH DERBY
Good catch, mate! It's all there,
Laurent. Of course, being kicked
out of the police force has made
you distrustful, eh? What was it, a
corruption charge? I do find it
hard to believe, I mean, look at
you! No matter, this should help
pay your bills, eh? Maybe even get
those teeth fixed. And that's only
the down payment, a hundred
thousand pounds. A good payday for
you.

MONSIEUR LAURENT
You promised two hundred!

ENGLISHMAN WITH DERBY
Patience. The remaining nine
hundred will be paid when the
Egyptian is dead. You know that,
ol' chap. That's the deal.

MONSIEUR LAURENT
Two hundred thousand *now* was our
deal!

ENGLISHMAN WITH DERBY
What can I do, mate? I just follow
orders. Speaking of which, Diana
and Dodi. They arrive in Paris in a
couple days, on Saturday the 30th.
They're booked at the Ritz. Be
there, Laurent. Do not muck this
up! Kill the Sphinx, with *this,* and
the rest of the money is yours.
Simple as that.

Englishman holds up camera-gun, aims it
squarely at Jacques. Its bulb flashes, a bullet
shoots, barely misses Jacques, who ducks. Just
in time.

                    ENGLISHMAN WITH DERBY (CONT'D)
               (to Jacques, laughs)
          Think you can handle this, boy?
               (to Skipper)
          Go!

The Hatteras' ENGINE ROARS to life as it speeds
away.

                    ENGLISHMAN WITH DERBY (CONT'D)
               (to Laurent, yells)
          And tell Monique to call me in
          London tonight. She will be the go-
          between.

EXT. HATTERAS YACHT - MOMENTS LATER

Englishman's flip cell phone RINGS. He answers
it.

                    ENGLISHMAN WITH DERBY
          Mission accomplished, sir.

                    GRAVELLY VOICE (V.O.)
          Not quite.

                    ENGLISHMAN WITH DERBY
          Pardon, but what--?

                    GRAVELLY VOICE (V.O.)
          I ask the questions. Just make sure
          your bloody ass is in Paris on the
          30th in case the frogs screw it up.

                    ENGLISHMAN WITH DERBY
          But sir, I have--

                    GRAVELLY VOICE (V.O.)
          You will be well compensated, I
          assure you. There's another million
          waiting for you with your name on
          it.

INT. GIFT SHOP, BUCKINGHAM PALACE - LATER - DAY

James and Ben watch a SALESMAN put a diamond
bangle bracelet onto Rhonda's wrist. She adores
it.

                    SALESMAN
          This diamond bracelet has been
          designed by the Crown Jeweler,
          special for the Lady Diana herself.

                    RHONDA
          Really! Honey?

                    JAMES
               (to Salesman)
          Such a bad habit. Calls all
          salesmen "honey."
               (to Rhonda)
          I like it, babe. It's so you.

Rhonda extends her braceleted hand, which James
caresses.

                    BEN
          Dad, will you just buy her the
          frickin' bracelet and let's go!

James shakes him a good-natured fist. Rhonda is
all smiles.

INT. HOTEL ROOM SUITE, LONDON - HOURS LATER -
NIGHT

Ben is sleeping. His bed is in an anteroom of
the suite.

Rhonda and James are in their bed, under the
covers. She reads Hello magazine. He finishes
writing a postcard.

                    RHONDA
          Who's that to?

                  JAMES
Me bruddah. "Queen Liz and Lady D
wish you were here. We Willis be in
Paris mañana. Tell Willis I'm ready
to work next week." Funny?

                  RHONDA
Sorta kinda... oh, James, I'm so
excited. *Gay Paree!*" They say it's
the most romantic city in the
world.

                  JAMES
I can show you some romance right
now, if you like. Yes, Madame
Beetch?

James turns to Rhonda and kisses her. She drops
her Hello magazine to the floor. He throws his
postcard in the air. They pull the covers over
their heads.

            RHONDA'S VOICE (V.O.)
Oooh, monsieur! Oh, jumbo Jimbo!

INT. WATERLOO TRAIN STATION, LONDON - NEXT DAY
- MORNING

    TITLE OVER: SAT., AUG. 30, 1997, 11:00 A.M.

The Goodrichs browse the concession stands.
Magazines and newspapers are rife with fuzzy
close-up photos of Princess Diana and Dodi Al
Fayed on their yacht.

MONIQUE, 65, sophisticated spy, dressed in
Chanel, stands near Paris departure gate. She
carries a handbag, an umbrella, and a miniature
apricot French poodle.

She kisses her TWIN GRANDCHILDREN, 10, and her
DAUGHTER, early 30's.

Englishman walks to Monique. He smartly hands
her a light blue shopping bag adorned with a
white satin ribbon. A beautifully wrapped gift
sticks out of the bag.

                    ENGLISHMAN WITH DERBY
                   (in French, whispers)
            Happy birthday, Monique darling.

He gives her a peck on the cheek, departs
quickly. Monique watches lovingly as he blends
into the crowd. Lost in love.

She suddenly glances at her watch.

                    MONIQUE
            Oh, I really must be going. Au
            revoir, mes chers enfants.

                    DAUGHTER
            Mother, who was that?

                    MONIQUE
            Just a friend, ma chérie. Isn't he
            dashing?

INT. EUROSTAR CHUNNEL TRAIN - HOURS LATER - DAY

The weather, bright and sunny.

Rhonda stares out window at moving landscape,
James reads a newspaper, Ben skims through a
Detective comic book.

Ben removes sweater, reveals Señor Frogs T-
shirt underneath.

                    RHONDA
            Are you kidding me?

                    BEN
            What?

                    RHONDA
        You can't wear that in France. Put
        your sweater back on.

Ben crosses his arms over chest, in defiance.

                    JAMES
        Hey, Pepé Le Pew, mind yer
        mamacita. Put the sweater back on.

                    BEN
        It's hot in here. I gotta pee.

Ben stands up, walks down the aisle.

Monique sits ten rows behind the Goodrichs. Ben
stops to pick up ribbon that has fallen near
her seat. He hands it to her.

His eyes fall on the camera-gun and a box of
bullets on her lap. She grabs the ribbon. The
poodle GROWLS.

                    MONIQUE
                  (in French)
        Thank you. Now leave us alone!

Ben runs the rest of the way down the aisle.

                    MONIQUE (CONT'D)
        Good doggie. Mummy loves you, oh,
        yes she does. Nyum nyum nyum.

INT. GARE DU NORD TRAIN STATION PLATFORM, PARIS
- LATER

    TITLE OVER: 2:00 P.M.

Englishman emerges stealthily from another
train car, runs up the stairs, disappears from
view.

> RHONDA
> The hotel has a shuttle. Hurry up,
> I'll grab us a place on line.

Rhonda and Ben exit train, a PORTER in tow.

James is saddled with two suitcases. He
accidentally bumps into Monique. She pokes him
sharply with her umbrella tip into the small of
his back. Ouch!

> MONIQUE
> Monsieur, you must be more careful.
> Imbécile. Aaagh, *Americans!*

James glares at her, rubs the small of his
back. The poodle SNARLS and BARKS at him.
Monique walks away in a huff.

> JAMES
> (to himself)
> Bienvenue.

EXT. NEAR CAR RENTAL AREA - MINUTES LATER

Englishman casually walks to a parked white
Fiat Uno. His key opens the trunk. He sees lots
of stuffed burlap bags and rips one open.

Large stacks of paper currency. Excellent! He
shuts the trunk, gets in the car, drives away.

EXT. TRAIN STATION PLAZA - SAME TIME

Very long cab and shuttle queue.

James walks onto plaza, luggage in hand. He
sees Rhonda and Ben across the street. James
joins them, then rubs the small of his back.

FRENCH LIMO DRIVER, 45, suave smooth talker, loads their luggage into black Mercedes limo's trunk. James is bemused.

                    RHONDA
          I am not standing on that line.

                    JAMES
               (indicates shuttle)
          But you said--

                    RHONDA
          You wanna stand on that line? I
          don't.

                    FRENCH LIMO DRIVER
          Three hundred fifty francs,
          monsieur. Plus tip. Fifteen minutes
          and whoosh, you are there.

                    JAMES
               (beat)
          Yep. When in Rome.

EXT. FRONT ENTRANCE, HOTEL VERITE - 15 MINUTES
LATER

     TITLE OVER: 3:15 P.M.

French Limo Driver unloads luggage.

EXT. LE BOURGET AIRPORT, NEAR PARIS - SAME TIME

     TITLE OVER: 3:15 P.M., LE BOURGET AIRPORT

Princess Diana and Dodi Al Fayed emerge from private jet. They enter a black Mercedes limo, whisking them away.

INT. RHONDA'S & JAMES'S ROOM, HOTEL VERITE -
MINUTES LATER

James and Ben nap, flopped out on top of king
bed. Rhonda unpacks all the bags. She's happy
to be in charge.

EXT. FRONT ENTRANCE, RITZ HOTEL - SAME TIME

Princess Diana and Dodi Al Fayed emerge from
limo. PAPARAZZI snap photos.

INT. RHONDA'S & JAMES'S ROOM - LATER - EARLY
EVENING

James talks on the hotel phone, sips martini.
An impatient Rhonda and Ben wait for him to
finish.

                    JAMES
          We're having an incredible time...
          yeah, be home in a few days...
          David, call the Willis people, I
          need that part... yes, and I need
          more auditions. I'm so ready for
          the big time, man. I'll move back
          to L.A., I'll do whatever it
          takes... I... wait... what?
               (looks at Rhonda)
          Gettin' the evil eye here, bro...
          okay, let the sightseeing begin.
          Make it so, Goodwrench!

James hangs up phone, chugs the drink. Rhonda
shakes her head, leads Ben out of room.

James pops a pill, shuts the door behind him.
Life is good.

INT. CONCIERGE DESK - MINUTES LATER

CONCIERGE, 40, bald, razor thin blond mustache, wears name tag "François." He shows the three Goodrichs a map.

>   CONCIERGE
>   I recommend the River Seine cruise,
>   madame. The City of Lights, so
>   breathtaking in the evening.

>   RHONDA
>   Sounds perfect. Um... *merci*?

>   CONCIERGE
>   *Merci* is correct! Okay, you will
>   catch your boat here, near the
>   Eiffel Tower. Do you see?

>   RHONDA
>   Yes. Oooh, I'm so excited.

Concierge gives map to Rhonda, escorts Goodrichs to door.

>   CONCIERGE
>   Just make a right turn out the
>   door. Follow the map. Ayez une
>   bonne nuit. Here, let me show you.

>   JAMES
>   (whispers)
>   What'd he just say?

Rhonda shrugs.

EXT. MAIN ENTRANCE, HOTEL VERITE - CONTINUOUS

They all exit hotel.

Rhonda surveys the street. She stares at some commotion to her left, diagonally across the street.

Concierge points right.

35

                    CONCIERGE
        That way, madame.

                    RHONDA
                (disregards Concierge)
        One sec. Wonder what's going on?

EXT. REAR ENTRANCE, RITZ HOTEL - CONTINUOUS

PAPARAZZI, camera equipment on many shoulders,
wait near motorcycles. Some sit restlessly on
the sidewalk.

Jacques holds camera-gun, paces back and forth.

Laurent, in police uniform, walks through
crowd. He wears the same Paris police cap on
his head, backward, with police badge affixed.

He passes near Jacques, who nods. Laurent
returns nod. Together they walk away from
crowd.

EXT. HOTEL VERITE - CONTINUOUS

                    BEN
        Maybe they're making a movie, dad.

James and Ben cross street.

Rhonda watches James take a flash photo of
crowd. The photo, by chance, includes Laurent
and Jacques in the foreground.

                    MONSIEUR LAURENT
                (in French)
        Hey! What the hell are you doing?
        You can't take pictures here!

                    RHONDA
        Guys, it's getting late. Come on.

James and Ben turn around mid-street, walk towards Rhonda.

Jacques hands camera-gun to Laurent. He runs after James, jumps on his back.

> JACQUES
> (in French)
> Give me that camera! You can't take pictures here.

James holds on to it solidly. They struggle.

> JAMES
> Get the hell off me. What are you, a fucking asshole?

James punches him, knocks him to the street, then places his 35mm camera securely in its belt-loop case.

James ushers Rhonda and Ben to quickly walk away, in direction originally indicated by Concierge.

EXT. REAR ENTRANCE, RITZ HOTEL - MOMENTS LATER

Princess Diana and Dodi Al Fayed emerge. Paparazzi cameras flash.

A black Mercedes limo pulls up. They enter the vehicle, it whisks them away.

Laurent approaches Jacques, helps him to his feet. Jacques starts to run after James. Laurent restrains him. They cross the street to the sidewalk.

Concierge watches from Hotel Vérité's front plaza.

                    JACQUES
We just blew it. Fuck! I'm going to
kill that American tourist
shithead. He just cost us a million
pounds. Now what?

                    MONSIEUR LAURENT
Easy, son. We will have other
opportunities to get Fayed. Right
now I want that film of his. I
cannot risk being photographed in
this uniform, especially next to
you. Walk away.

                    JACQUES
But papa, I must ask. Why do you
keep insisting on wearing it?

                    MONSIEUR LAURENT
Old habits die hard, Jacques. In
truth, I cannot help myself.

Concierge approaches Laurent.

                    CONCIERGE
Officer, is everything okay? Those
Americans are guests at my hotel.

                    MONSIEUR LAURENT
Did you speak to them? Do you know
where they're off to?

                    CONCIERGE
I am not really certain, but--

Concierge observes Laurent discreetly offer him
a large wad of bills. Concierge hastily takes
the cash, pockets it.

                    CONCIERGE (CONT'D)
                (the light bulb goes on)
Ah, the Goodrichs, of course. A
lovely family. Well, they will be
cruising the River Seine tonight, I

am certain of that. I suggested
they buy their tickets near the
Eiffel Tower. Are they in trouble?

Laurent shakes his head. He walks away with
Jacques, dials his cell phone. It RINGS.

> MONIQUE'S VOICE (V.O.)
> Have you taken out the Sphinx?

> MONSIEUR LAURENT
> We've run into a snag.
> (beat)
> Monique, call the boys. Jacques is
> with me. Tell Rémy and Pierre we
> must have a family meeting now. A
> new plan. We'll be home shortly.

EXT. VARIOUS PARIS STREETS - LATER - TWILIGHT

The Goodrichs stand near the Egyptian Obelisk
in the center square. Rhonda looks at map,
points west. James and Ben follow her gaze to
reveal the distant Eiffel Tower.

James snaps a few photos. Ben puts on his
Walkman ear phones. Rhonda leads the charge as
she points to a sign for an underground subway.

EXT. FERRYBOAT TICKET BOOTH, REAR - SAME TIME

Monique surveys surrounding area. Deserted. She
knocks on door. TICKET BOOTH GIRL, young,
petite, long yellow scarf around her neck,
opens it with a smile.

Monique pulls out a damp blue rag, covers
Ticket Booth Girl's face. She collapses,
unconscious. Monique pushes her into booth,
joins her inside, shuts door.

EXT. EIFFEL TOWER - HOURS LATER - NIGHT

TOURIST takes photo of the Goodrichs.

Illuminated sign on Eiffel Tower reads "L'anni 2000: 854."

EXT. FERRYBOAT DOCK - MINUTES LATER

They sit. James and Ben yawn. Rhonda looks at her watch.

> JAMES
> Honey, the Benster and I are pooped and it's gettin' chilly so what say we do this thing tomorrow night?

> RHONDA
> Jim, I'm going on that cruise with or without you. We've only got three nights.

> JAMES
> Alright, lemme get los billetes.

A throng of FRENCH PASSENGERS board the ferryboat.

EXT. FERRYBOAT TICKET BOOTH, FRONT - MOMENTS LATER

James approaches ticket booth cage. He puts his open wallet, face up, on counter. He holds up three fingers.

Monique stands in booth behind thick vertical bars. She wears Ticket Booth Girl's long yellow scarf.

> JAMES
> I want to buy, um, trois tickets. Hey, aren't you--?

                    MONIQUE
          Forty francs each, monsieur.

He gives her money, she gives him three tickets
and change. He counts the change.

                    JAMES
          Wait, you made a mistake. I think.
          You look familiar, were you on the--

                    BEN (O.S.)
          C'mon dad, hurry up!

                    MONIQUE
          It is the correct fiat exchange,
          Monsieur Goodrich.

                    JAMES
          How do you know my name?

She points to open wallet.

                    MONIQUE
          American. Express!

He sees his American Express card is face up,
his name in full view. He puts the wallet back
in his pocket.

                    JAMES
          Right. Were you the lady on--?

                    RHONDA (O.S.)
          Let's go already.

                    MONIQUE
              (in French)
          Get on your boat. It is about to
          depart. We are sold out!

She slams down the cage bars.

Ben joins James as he counts his change again.

>   JAMES
> Just a minute. Oh wait, I was
> thinking English *pounds*. Right, I
> gave her two hundred *francs* and--

Ferryboat's FOGHORN blows.

>   BEN
> Good one, dad.

James turns to see ferryboat departing.

INT. FERRYBOAT TICKET BOOTH - 1 HOUR LATER

Monique watches the Goodrichs through a small
crack. They are first in line to embark.

She dials her cell phone, which displays 11:05
P.M.

>   MONIQUE
>   (in French)
> They will be back from the cruise
> in exactly one hour, my sweet Rémy.

>   RÉMY'S VOICE (V.O.)
> And I'll be waiting dock side,
> mother. Trust me, I *will* get his
> camera. Even if I have to kill him.

EXT. FERRYBOAT DOCK - 1 HOUR LATER

TITLE OVER: SUN., AUG. 31, 1997, 12:05 A.M.

The ferryboat docks. The Goodrichs and
PASSENGERS disembark.

A sleepy Ben recognizes Monique talking on cell
phone outside the ticket booth. He keeps it to
himself.

<table>
<tr><td>

LOUDSPEAKER (V.O.)
Nous vous remercions
de votre patronage et
vous souhaitons une
soirée plaisante.
Soyez nuit sûre et et
bonne.
</td><td>

JAMES
(to Rhonda)
Very educational, mon
ami. We didn't
understand a woid.
</td></tr>
</table>

             RHONDA
Well, I thought it was amazing, Mr.
Romance. A wonderful ending to a
fantastic day. Thank you, boys.

She kisses James smack on the lips, musses up
Ben's hair.

James runs ahead of his family, snaps a photo
of them.

EXT. EIFFEL TOWER - MOMENTS LATER

James sees an empty taxi. Sign in the
windshield: Réservé. The taxi's engine IDLES
and its headlights are on.

             JAMES
How lucky are we? Come on!

REMY, early 20's, is on his flip cell, next to
driver's door.

EXT. REMY'S TAXI - MOMENTS LATER

The Goodrichs approach. Rémy, still on his
cell, signals "just a moment," removes Réservé
sign.

Illuminated sign on Eiffel Tower reads "L'anni
2000: 853."

                    MONIQUE'S VOICE (V.O.)
          (in French)
     ...and stay away from the Pont de
     l'Alma. We have big business there
     tonight. Just get his camera.

Rémy rolls his eyes.

                    RÉMY
     I know all about it, mother. Ciao.

INT. REMY'S TAXI - 2 MINUTES LATER

Rémy in driver's seat. Ben in rear, between his
parents.

                    RÉMY
     Where to?

                    RHONDA
     Our hotel, the, um... Hotel Vérité.
     I forget the exact address. It's
     one of those boutique hotels.
          (the light bulb goes on)
     Oh wait. It's next to the House of
     Dior, or Chanel, something like
     that... on the Rue Cambon.

Rhonda takes out her map, shows him. James
takes his camera out of its case. Rémy lights a
cigarette.

                    RHONDA (CONT'D)
     My hotel is... oh, here it is,
     right here. The Hotel Vérité!

                    JAMES
     Hey, Ben? One more shot?

                    BEN
          (sleepily grumpy)
     No more tonight, dad. Please!

44

Rémy's taxi pulls away from curb, fast, with a
SCREECH.

          JAMES
   Whoa! Easy, cowboy!

EXT. REAR ENTRANCE, RITZ HOTEL - MINUTES LATER

   TITLE OVER: 12:19 A.M.

HENRI PAUL, 41, stands near driver's door of
black Mercedes limo. He stares at THIRTY
PAPARAZZI who have assembled. Some sit on
motorcycles, some sit in cars, some pace
anxiously.

A white Fiat Uno, driven by Englishman, slowly
cruises alongside, and then past, Henri.

Englishman scans crowd of Paparazzi. He spots
Laurent and Jacques standing alone, several
dozen feet away.

Fiat pulls alongside Laurent and Jacques, then
stops.

EXT. RUE CAMBON - MOMENTS LATER

       ENGLISHMAN WITH DERBY
  What the bloody hell are you doing?

        JACQUES
  Too many people. I'll never get a
  clear shot.

       MONSIEUR LAURENT
  The plan is... il est ridicule.

> ENGLISHMAN WITH DERBY
> You know, this is the second time
> today you screwed up. Jump in.
> Let's bloody well make this happen!

Jacques, camera-gun at the ready, eagerly gets
into front passenger seat. Laurent climbs into
rear seat.

EXT. REAR ENTRANCE, RITZ HOTEL - MOMENTS LATER

Paparazzi snap lots of photos.

Princess Diana exits hotel, covers her face
with her hands.

TREVOR REES-JONES, 29, Princess Diana's
bodyguard, escorts her to waiting black
Mercedes. He opens rear passenger door, she
enters, he SLAMS door shut.

Trevor swiftly enters black Mercedes via right
front passenger door, SLAMS it shut.

Dodi exits hotel, makes a beeline for black
Mercedes. Henri swiftly opens rear driver's
side door. Dodi gets inside.

> HENRI
> (to Paparazzi, taunts)
> Catch us if you can!

Henri kicks Dodi's door shut, laughs at crowd,
ambles towards the driver's door, gets in,
SLAMS his door shut.

Black Mercedes departs fast, with a LOUD
SCREECH.

Some Paparazzi REV their motorcycles, some REV
their car engines. A few Paparazzi SPEAK into
flip cell phones.

Eight motorcycles, one black car follow black
Mercedes in close pursuit.

EXT. BLACK MERCEDES - CONTINUOUS

Black Mercedes speeds erratically down Rue
Cambon. It passes the front entrance of Hotel
Vérité, on the right.

At street's end, black Mercedes makes a right,
then a sharp left at Place de la Concorde.
Tires SCREECH.

Black Mercedes begins to make a right onto the
Champs Elyssees but a parked green car blocks
egress. Black Mercedes almost hits that parked
green car.

Fiat, parked across the street from the parked
green car, comes to life. Fiat's engine REVS,
its headlights go on. It tailgates the black
Mercedes. The chase has begun.

INT. TRAFFIC VIDEO CONTROL CENTRAL - MOMENTS
LATER

A bank of twenty closed-circuit TV monitors and
VCRs, in a cramped, smoky office, displays live
traffic conditions in the tunnels of Paris.

CONTROL BOOTH MAN, 50, smokes a cigarette,
phone to ear, listens keenly.

The only light in the room comes from the TV
monitors.

INT. WHITE FIAT UNO - MOMENTS LATER

Englishman yells into his flip cell phone.

                    ENGLISHMAN WITH DERBY
                 (in French)
            Cut the video. Now!

INT. TRAFFIC VIDEO CONTROL CENTRAL - CONTINUOUS

Control Booth Man perks up, flips a switch.
Monitors go dark.

                    CONTROL BOOTH MAN
            C'est fait.

The burning cigarette ember is the only light
in the room.

INT. BLACK MERCEDES - 2 MINUTES LATER

Henri looks in rearview mirror, grimaces. He
sees the Fiat, followed closely by two more
cars and several motorcycles. The chase is in
full earnest.

                    HENRI
            Shit!

Henri presses the pedal to the metal. Trevor
buckles his seatbelt.

EXT. BLACK MERCEDES - CONTINUOUS

The speeding black Mercedes SCREECHES as it
makes the next available right, heading west.
It races along at 95 kph (60 mph) in the right
lane towards Alma Tunnel.

Two motorcycles approach Henri's door. One
comes very close to right rear passenger door.

Fiat continues to tailgate. It gets closer.

INT. BLACK MERCEDES, WESTBOUND - CONTINUOUS

Princess Diana's face is masked in shadow. Her delicate hand tightly clasps Dodi's.

> DODI
> Speed it up, Henri! Let's lose these assholes.

INT. REMY'S TAXI, EASTBOUND - MOMENTS LATER

Cigarette smoke in the speeding taxi gets thicker. Rhonda coughs, chokes. She and James crank open the rear windows.

> JAMES
> Put the cigarette out, man!

Rémy curses under his breath, throws the cigarette out the window. Now he's pissed. He presses the pedal to the metal.

Rhonda searches frantically for a seatbelt, to no avail.

> BEN
> Dad! This guy is nuts.

> JAMES
> You're freaking my family out, man! Slow the fuck down!

Rémy turns around to face them.

> RÉMY
> (in French)
> You want my first born, too?

> JAMES
> Watch out. Jesus fuck!

Rémy turns back to the steering wheel, barely avoiding...

EXT. REMY'S TAXI, EASTBOUND - CONTINUOUS

   TITLE OVER: 12:21 A.M.

...crashing into a red car.

Taxi speeds along the avenue. From out of
nowhere a blue car swerves, cuts off taxi. Taxi
brakes hard. Blue car hits Taxi's upper front
fender, near tire.

Blue car swerves away to the right, takes exit
ramp.

Taxi develops a flat tire but keeps moving. It
can now only follow the roadway eastbound,
becoming part of a traffic jam leading inside
the Alma Tunnel.

INT. REMY'S TAXI, EASTBOUND - MOMENTS LATER

                    RÉMY
             (in French, to himself)
         Shit. She's gonna kill me.

Blue emergency lights flash from inside tunnel,
reflecting on tunnel walls up ahead. Taxi moves
very slowly now.

          RHONDA   BEN
      Thank God.   What's goin' on, Dad?

                    JAMES
                 (whispers)
         He should be locked up is what's
         goin' on. Crazy señor frog.

Rémy's eyes narrow. He looks at James
menacingly in rearview mirror.

EXT. BLACK MERCEDES IN TUNNEL (WEST) - SAME
TIME

Black Mercedes veers into left lane, speeds up into tunnel. No traffic ahead or behind.

Fiat, eight motorcycles, three other cars follow. A very frightened Diana looks out black Mercedes' rear window.

Black Mercedes passes a parked police car, its blue emergency lights flashing. TWO TUNNEL POLICEMEN stand nearby, speak to each other nonchalantly. Their police car blocks egress for any other westbound traffic, of which there is none.

Fiat rams black Mercedes' rear. Diana and Dodi jolt forward.

EXT. INSIDE THE TUNNEL - MOMENTS LATER

Taxi in heavy traffic. Flat tire getting flatter.

A few hundred feet ahead of taxi is RED BEARDED PAPARAZZI. He stands in eastbound lane, scans westbound oncoming traffic.

He sees black Mercedes coming, selects "Rapid Flash" setting on his camera, takes photos of black Mercedes as it approaches.

The bursts of light from his camera flashes are incessant.

INT. REMY'S TAXI IN TUNNEL (EAST) - MOMENTS LATER

James points his camera at Ben.

      JAMES   BEN
   Surprise!   Dad! Are you kidding?

Ben lunges for James's camera, pushes its aim outside taxi. It points into oncoming western lane of tunnel traffic.

They each stubbornly refuse to let go.

EXT. INSIDE THE TUNNEL - SAME TIME

Red Bearded Paparazzi's camera flashes several dozen times.

Taxi and black Mercedes are about to pass each other.

INT. BLACK MERCEDES IN TUNNEL (WEST) - SAME TIME

Henri is distracted by bursts of camera flashes. He turns his head in that direction.

INT. REMY'S TAXI IN TUNNEL (EAST) - SAME TIME

Rémy looks in rearview mirror. He sees James and Ben holding their camera as it flashes once, pointed at black Mercedes.

                    BEN
          Enough with the pictures. Here!

Ben releases camera to James.

James and Rémy see four faces from the emitted camera flashes. In the black Mercedes: Henri Paul driving. In the Fiat: Englishman driving, Jacques in front, Laurent in rear.

EXT. INSIDE THE TUNNEL - MOMENTS LATER

Red Bearded Paparazzi's camera flashes light up the tunnel.

INT. WHITE FIAT UNO IN TUNNEL (WEST) - MOMENTS
LATER

Laurent sees Rémy driving the taxi.

> MONSIEUR LAURENT
> (in French, to Jacques)
> What the hell is your nitwit
> brother doing here?

INT. BLACK MERCEDES IN TUNNEL (WEST) - MOMENTS
LATER

EXT. BLACK MERCEDES IN TUNNEL (WEST) - MOMENTS
LATER

Henri turns his head away from camera flashes.

Black Mercedes' rear bumper endures two more
sharp jolts from Fiat. Fiat speeds up, now
parallel to black Mercedes' driver's door.

INT. WHITE FIAT UNO IN TUNNEL (WEST) -
CONTINUOUS

Jacques opens Fiat's window, aims camera-gun at
Henri. The camera flash goes off, the gun
portion jams. No bullets.

> ENGLISHMAN WITH DERBY
> Stupid fucking bugger! You only
> pressed the *flash* button. You have
> to hold the *gun* button, too. I told
> you--

Fiat moves ahead of black Mercedes, then
deliberately slows down. Black Mercedes hits
left rear taillight of Fiat, breaking it.

Fiat exits Alma Tunnel.

INT. BLACK MERCEDES IN TUNNEL (WEST) -
CONTINUOUS

Henri slams on brakes. Black Mercedes skids,
tires SCREECH.

```
     DODI          DIANA          TREVOR
   Diana!       Oh my God!      Watch out!
```

EXT. BLACK MERCEDES IN TUNNEL (WEST) -
CONTINUOUS

Black Mercedes rebounds against right-hand
tunnel wall for thirty feet. Then it spins on
the road surface in a 180 degree turn.

It smashes into a concrete pillar, travelling
another 90 degrees.

It collides into tunnel wall with a deafening
CRASH.

HORN BLARES for ten seconds. Then, deafening
SILENCE.

EXT. REMY'S TAXI IN TUNNEL (EAST) - MOMENTS
LATER

Rémy steps on brake, comes to a complete stop.
Taxi is about twenty feet away from black
Mercedes wreckage.

Rémy extends upper half of his body through his
open window, craning his torso and neck to get
the best view of carnage.

Paparazzi quickly converge on decimated black
Mercedes.

EXT. INSIDE THE TUNNEL - MOMENTS LATER

Red Bearded Paparazzi crosses roadway, wedges
himself between tunnel wall and wreckage. He
takes more photos.

Paparazzi cameras shoot flash photos of demolished black Mercedes from every conceivable angle.

INT. REMY'S TAXI IN TUNNEL (EAST) - CONTINUOUS

The Goodrichs stare in horror.

         JAMES   RHONDA   BEN
       Jesus!   Oh my God!   Holy crap!

Rémy crosses himself, the top half of his body still hanging out his window.

                    RÉMY
              (smiles, to himself)
         C'est la vie. C'est la mort.

EXT. INSIDE THE TUNNEL - MOMENTS LATER

Ten motorcycles are parked on cement median strip.

Two Tunnel Policemen continue to calmly stand near parked police car, watching Paparazzi. Their car's blue emergency lights continue to flash.

INT. REMY'S TAXI IN TUNNEL (EAST) - 1 MINUTE LATER

Traffic ahead begins to move. Rémy resumes driving.

The Goodrichs stare at the black Mercedes wreckage.

                    RHONDA
         Oh my God. Look, there's a woman in
         that car.

                    BEN
          Where, mom?

Rhonda points out the window.

                    RHONDA
          Right over there. Oh my God.

          JAMES   BEN
Where you looking? I   How'd the cops get
don't--   here so fast?

                    RHONDA (CONT'D)
          She's not moving. She might be
          dead. Oh my God.

                    JAMES
          What's with all the photos? Is this
          how they do forensics in France?

EXT. REMY'S TAXI - MINUTES LATER

No cars at all in sight.

Taxi moves forward, almost on its tire rim, as
it limps out of Tunnel. It parks near Egyptian
Obelisk.

INT. REMY'S TAXI - CONTINUOUS

Rémy turns around.

                    RÉMY
          Crazy frog? Give me your camera,
          you American shit. My brother asked
          you nice but maybe not nice enough
          so I offer five hundred pounds. You
          keep the camera, just give me the
          film. It is a deal more than fair,
          yes?

Rémy tries to grab camera. James puts camera in its case.

> JAMES
> Deal this, shit for brains! Rhon,
> Ben, get out. Now! Go!

Rhonda and Ben make a fast exit via Rhonda's door.

James opens his door. Taxi pulls away fast, flat tire now rimming it. James dangles out his door, half-in half-out.

EXT. REMY'S TAXI - CONTINUOUS

> RHONDA   BEN
> Oh my God. James!   Dad! Jump!

James jumps, rolls onto the street, rolls over, stands up, pants ripped, scrapes on face.

Taxi shifts into reverse. It gains speed, aims for James. He jumps out of the way. Just in time.

> JAMES
> I'm okay. Run! To the hotel!

Rhonda and Ben race down the street. James follows. Taxi hobbles away in the opposite direction.

> SMASH CUT TO:

INT. REMY'S TAXI - MINUTES LATER

Rémy, on his flip cell phone, holds it away from his ear.

> MONIQUE'S VOICE (V.O.)
> Imbécile!

INT. RHONDA'S & JAMES'S ROOM - MINUTES LATER

The Goodrichs, out of breath.

Ben sits in armchair, stares into space, unresponsive. James lays down on king bed.

>   RHONDA
>   What the hell was that about?
>   Jamie, you okay?

James smiles, gives a feeble "hang loose," tries to sit up.

>   JAMES
>   Hunky-dory, Lori.

>   RHONDA
>   I'm gonna call the police.

James winces. He takes off a shoe, falls back onto king bed.

>   JAMES
>   The police were *there*, for Christ's
>   sake. I'm wiped. Let's just go to
>   bed.

James starts to drift off. Ben walks to his own room.

>   JAMES (CONT'D)
>   Put the camera in the...

Rhonda walks to wall safe with camera.

>   BEN (O.S.)
>   Getting way too creepy for me.
>   Bullet lady, train. Bullet lady,
>   ferry--

>   RHONDA
>   Bullet lady? What're you...?

She puts the camera down on a table near the
safe.

                    RHONDA (CONT'D)
          Ben?

                    BEN (O.S.)
          Nothing, mom. 'Night. 'Night, dad.

Rhonda walks to James, lays down on the bed
next to him.

                    RHONDA
               (whispers in his ear)
          Hold me, honey. I'm scared.

James SNORES softly, turns over. Sound asleep.

Rhonda gets up, puts camera in safe, takes off
his other shoe, lays down next to him again.
Holds him tightly.

                    RHONDA (CONT'D)
               (whispers)
          Jamie, let's get out of here. Let's
          go home.

James SNORES louder.

END OF ACT I.

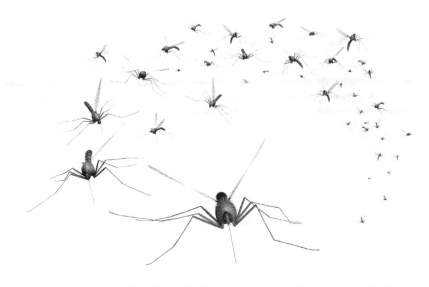

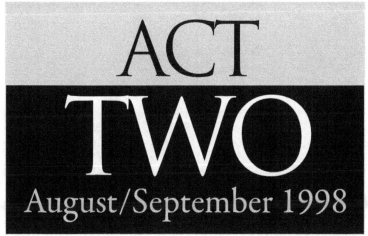

ACT
TWO
August/September 1998

Paris

INT. RESTAURANT, HOTEL VERITE - 9 HOURS LATER -
MORNING

                TITLE OVER 10:30 A.M.

Eerie SILENCE in restaurant, except for RATTLE
of cutlery and CLINKING of fine china.
CUSTOMERS sit somberly.

The Goodrichs finish breakfast. James has
scrapes on arms, small bandage on forehead. Ben
listens to his Walkman.

                    JAMES
          Rhonda, stop it already, it's a
          nonrefundable package. Hotel,
          airlines, the whole caboodle. It
          would cost--

                    RHONDA
          But what do they even think you
          have pictures *of*? Let's get the
          hell out of here or tell the police
          or--

                    JAMES
          Hey! You think I'm gonna let some
          assholes ruin this trip? Chill out,
          mommy. Really. Big Jimmy can handle
          it.
               (scoffs)
          So concerned about me.

                    RHONDA
          I'm concerned about *us*, moron. And
          do not berate me like that.
               (beat)
          Creep.

Rhonda stands up.

>   BEN
> Stop it. Both of you. I can't
> listen to this.

He runs out of the restaurant.

>   JAMES
> Way to score, babe, a three-pointer
> for sure... not. Hey, you wanted
> Paris, you got Paris. Go home?
> You're really too much sometimes,
> you know that?

James stands up, approaches Rhonda.

>   JAMES (CONT'D)
> We are going sightseeing like you,
> like *we* planned, okay? Oh man, I
> got a mother of a headache. You got
> any aspirin, babe? What museum was
> it again, honey?

He puts his arm around her. She moves away from
him.

>   RHONDA
> The Louvre. I'll be up soon.

James tries to kiss her on the cheek. She
pushes past him.

>   RHONDA (CONT'D)
> Conversation finished. Walking away
> now.

INT. CONCIERGE DESK - MOMENTS LATER

Concierge sees an upset Rhonda approach. He
smiles brightly, selects a small envelope,
holds it out for her.

                    CONCIERGE
          Madame Goodrich, your museum
          passes. And, I have made for you
          the dinner reservations you
          requested for tonight, at eight.

                    RHONDA
          Great.

She takes envelope from him.

                    RHONDA (CONT'D)
          François, I need you to arrange an
          English speaking driver for us, one
          who doesn't smoke. We had this
          lunatic cabbie last night, nearly
          got us killed.

                    CONCIERGE
          Oh madame, I am so sorry to hear--

                    RHONDA
          And we saw this horrible car crash,
          in a tunnel somewhere. I saw a lady
          who I think was killed--

                    CONCIERGE
          Madame, I must apologize for asking
          this but, where did you say you
          picked up this taxi?

                    RHONDA
          At the Eiffel Tower. We were coming
          back from that cruise and... oh! He
          tried to rob us, he tried to run my
          husband down with--

                    CONCIERGE
          What time was this at?

                    RHONDA
          After midnight sometime, around
          twelve-thirty, I think. It was so--

The Concierge cocks his head.

> CONCIERGE
> Do you know which tunnel?

> RHONDA
> (beat)
> Which... how would I... why?

> CONCIERGE
> Madame, then you did not hear.

Rhonda's brow furrows, she stares at him in silence. She sits down in nearby chair.

> CONCIERGE (CONT'D)
> The woman you saw in the car? It was the Lady D. The Princess.

> RHONDA
> Who... what? Is she-- is she okay?

> CONCIERGE
> Madame. I am so sorry to tell you. The Princess Diana. She is dead.

Color drains from Rhonda's face. She attempts to stand up, loses balance, grabs ahold of the desk.

INT. BEN'S BEDROOM - SAME TIME

Ben lays on his bed, watches TV. He suddenly sits up, laughs.

> BEN
> Dad! It's your Coke commercial. In French. Ya gotta see this. Quick!

James rushes into Ben's room, toothbrush in hand. They watch the rest of his commercial. MTV comes back on the air.

>   JAMES
>   That was great, dude, good score.
>   Two bonus points for that one.

James returns to his room.

>   JAMES'S VOICE (O.C.)
>   Yo Benster, find some news. Let's
>   see what's happening back home.

Ben picks up remote control, stops at BBC News
Channel.

>   WOMAN AIDS ACTIVIST (ON TV)
>   Princess Diana had a great concern
>   and showed a real love for the
>   children with AIDS.

>   HOST (ON TV)
>   How do you think this will affect
>   that work?

>   WOMAN AIDS ACTIVIST (ON TV)
>   She will be sorely missed...

James re-enters Ben's room, sits down on the
bed.

>   JAMES   WOMAN AIDS
>   What's this?   ACTIVIST (ON TV)
>   ...but the AIDS work
>   for the children will
>   go on. Princess Diana
>   carried a message of
>   hope to those
>   children, on a
>   greater scale than
>   anyone else has ever
>   done.

TV picture cuts to photo of Princess Diana,
with subtitle: **"Princess Diana, 1961 - 1997."**
James and Ben stare at each other, then stare
back at the TV, dumbfounded.

BEN	JAMES
What? Princess Diana	Shh! Shh! Oh my God,
died? Did she have	I can't believe this!
AIDS and no one knew	Shh! Listen!
about it?	

TV cuts to live video coverage of black
Mercedes wreckage clean-up effort. Another
subtitle: **"Princess Diana, Dead in Paris."**

> HOST (ON TV)
> To repeat, tragic breaking news
> from France, shocking the world.
> Princess Diana was killed early
> this morning in an automobile
> accident in Paris.

> JAMES
> Oh my God. Listen, kid, when mom
> comes up we gotta make sure she's
> sitting down first. This will--

Suite door UNLOCKS. Rhonda, in a daze, walks to
door jamb at Ben's room. James MUTES the TV.

Rhonda holds an aspirin vial.

> RHONDA
> Here's your aspirin. Princess--

> BEN
> We just heard.

Rhonda fumbles aspirin vial. It falls to floor,
aspirin tablets SCATTERING. Ben UNMUTES the TV.

> HOST (ON TV)
> While we are just now getting
> information on what happened in the
> underpass, there are some early
> reports about Diana's car being
> chased by local paparazzi.

James hurries to her side, walks her slowly to
Ben's bed. She sits down, watches TV.

James gets on the floor, cleans up aspirin
mess. He chews four tablets, then turns his
attention back to the TV.

INT. REMY'S TAXI IN TUNNEL (EAST) - NIGHT
(JAMES'S FLASHBACK)

The camera, in James's and Ben's hands, flashes
once, pointing at black Mercedes.

                    BEN
Enough with the pictures. Here!

Ben releases camera to James.

INT. BEN'S BEDROOM - MOMENTS LATER - MORNING

          JAMES   HOST (ON TV)
       (to himself)   The entire nation of
      Oh no. Shit.   Great Britain, along
                           with the rest--

James is distressed. He presses MUTE button on
remote.

                    RHONDA
What are you doing? I wanna hear--

James stares at TV screen.

                  RHONDA (CONT'D)
We have to go to the police.

                    JAMES
Not again. Stop.

                    RHONDA
We have to tell them what we saw.

Rhonda grabs remote from James. She UNMUTES the TV.

                    RHONDA (CONT'D)
          Oh my God, look. Shh!

                    HOST (ON TV)
          ...and we have reports from the
          royal family that Prince Charles
          will be in Paris within the next
          few hours, en route to hospital.
          Speculation is--

James takes remote back and MUTES the TV.

                    RHONDA
          Did you hear that? Let's go to the
          hospital and tell Prince Charles
          what we saw. He'll want to hear
          about the papara--

                    JAMES
          Yeah, let's tell the Queen, too.
          Come on, let's get outta here. You
          have those Louvre tickets, right?

Rhonda nods. She is fixated by the TV.

James holds down a camera button until it
CLICKS. He removes the film roll and pockets
it. He walks to TV, shuts it off.

He walks to the suite door. Ben joins him.

                    BEN
          Dad's right. Come on, mom.

                    RHONDA
          We can't keep quiet about this.

                    JAMES
          I'm Fedexing the film to David, I
          wanna know what's on it. Let's go.

INT. LOUVRE MUSEUM - LATER - AFTERNOON

James and Rhonda, arm-in-arm, walk slowly
through museum. Ben stops to look at Van Gogh's
"Starry Night" nearby.

                    RHONDA
          Be right back. Bathroom.

Rhonda walks away. James sneaks a pill and a
flask swig.

INT. LADIES' BATHROOM DOOR - MOMENTS LATER

Rhonda stands on line. GERMAN WOMAN is at front
of line. Behind her are ASIAN WOMAN, BRITISH
WOMAN, Rhonda, and Monique, holding poodle.

                    BRITISH WOMAN
          It was a conspiracy. The royals
          didn't like this whole Dodi thing,
          not at all. Believe me, I know.

                    ASIAN WOMAN
          A conspiracy? You really think so?

                    GERMAN WOMAN
          I heard the police did nothing to
          help her. That she was pregnant and
          they just left her there to die.

TWO WOMEN exit bathroom. German Woman, Asian
Woman enter.

                    RHONDA
          What's the difference how she died?
          What about her children, growing up
          without their mother now? What
          about Dodi's father?

ANOTHER WOMAN exits bathroom.

RHONDA (CONT'D)
What's wrong with you people?

BRITISH WOMAN
You know, there's talk about the
paparazzi chasing them. They can be
brutes. Why, this could be a murder
case and not an accident at all. I
even heard they're looking for
witnesses.

British Woman holds door open for her. Rhonda
just stands there, lost in thought.

RHONDA
(to Monique)
After you.

MONIQUE
Merci.

Monique enters bathroom. Rhonda stays put.

British Woman looks at Rhonda curiously, then
leaves her there, and enters bathroom herself.

INT. LOUVRE MUSEUM - SEVERAL MINUTES LATER

Rhonda rejoins James. Ben studies a nearby
sculpture.

RHONDA
Why do you look so paranoid?

He looks over his shoulders.

JAMES
(whispers)
The flash from my camera, I think
it caused the crash. And the creep
who attacked me on the street? The
cabbie said that was his brother.
You know, the more I think about--

Ben walks to them.

>   RHONDA
>   (holds back laughter)
>   Wait, lemme get this straight. You
>   think you caused the crash?

>   BEN
>   Mom, please don't start.

Ben rolls his eyes, walks away to look at "Mona
Lisa."

>   JAMES
>   That's why I wanna keep our big
>   mouths shut. We might be lambs to
>   the slaughter here. No, there's no
>   way we can go to the police with
>   this, I don't wanna be framed. If
>   the cabbie tells them where we're
>   staying, then--

>   RHONDA
>   Framed? You mean like Wodger
>   Wabbit? Oh James, you do crack me
>   up.

>   JAMES
>   (whispers)
>   Will you shut up! If they think my
>   camera flash blinded that driver,
>   we're *all* in deep shit.

>   RHONDA
>   *You* shut up. Have another drink,
>   Mr. Cloak And Dagger. Look at me.
>   Nobody's eyeing you with suspicion,
>   Jim. You're an unemployed actor, a
>   nobody.
>   (laughs wretchedly)
>   *Framed!* That's a thigh-slapper!

James turns away from her. She tries to kiss
him.

                    RHONDA (CONT'D)
Oh come on, Jamie. I'm sorry, it's
just that... my turn, okay? I
apologize. Oh, don't be so--

                    JAMES
Walking away now. Creep.

He storms away from her. Ben watches in dismay.

EXT. PARIS STREET - 1 HOUR LATER - LATE
AFTERNOON

The Goodrichs walk down the street. Rhonda sees
mustached FRENCH POLICEMAN #1, billy club in
hand, standing on the corner watching the
traffic flow.

                    RHONDA
I hope he understands English.

Rhonda and Ben walk away from James, approach
French Policeman #1. James watches from a short
distance away.

                    RHONDA (CONT'D)
Officer, we witnessed Diana's
accident last night. We want to
tell police investigators what we
saw.

French Policeman #1 smiles reassuringly.

     RHONDA (CONT'D)   BEN
Wait. We were in the   We... were...
tunnel.   *witnesses*.

                    FRENCH POLICEMAN #1
I understand, madame, young
monsieur, but we have enough
witnesses.

James approaches.

                    RHONDA
Wait. You have enough *what*?

                    FRENCH POLICEMAN #1
We have enough witnesses. Now,
excusez-moi.

French Policeman #1 walks away.

                    RHONDA
Enough witnesses? It was like, like
he was trying to get rid of us.

James scoffs, takes a big swig.

                    JAMES
Anybody home yet?

INT. RHONDA'S & JAMES'S ROOM - LATER - DUSK

Rhonda, James and Ben dress for dinner. A TV is
on.

                    NEWSCASTER (ON TV)
There is still a lot of speculation
about how Princess Diana's car
crash occurred. We are trying to
find out how long it took the
ambulance to get to the Alma Tunnel
and how long it took to transport
Princess Diana and Dodi Al Fayed to
hospital. And there are reports
that a white Fiat Uno was involved.

James's eyes widen as he looks at TV screen.

                    NEWSCASTER (ON TV) (CONT'D)
If so, who was driving it? And to
what extent did the paparazzi
interfere?

EXT. LE VAUDEVILLE RESTAURANT - LATER - NIGHT

WAITER #1 serves dessert to Goodrichs at outdoor table adjacent to street.

Two American couples, SPENCER & JOHN and HOPE & ALAN, sit together at nearby table.

                    HOPE
             (to Rhonda)
          So you arrived from England
          yesterday?

Rhonda nods.

                    SPENCER
          You must really be in shock.

                    HOPE
          It's all anybody can talk about.

                    ALAN
          Our son called us from Jersey, in
          the middle of the night there. At
          first he thought it was some
          outlandish skit on Saturday Night
          Live or something, and then--

                    BEN
          We saw the crash. We were there.

James puts hand to head, takes a big chug of drink.

                    JOHN
          My God, you were in the tunnel?

                    RHONDA
          It was awful. We're debating
          whether to tell the police.

James sees a white Fiat Uno moving slowly down the street. It stops nearby. Laurent is in rear seat, staring at James. James rubs his eyes, looks back. The Fiat has moved on.

            SPENCER
Debating? You have to.

            ALAN
I think so.

            BEN
We tried to.

            JAMES
     (to Spencer, slurs)
You're right. It's our civical
duty. Civic. Rhonda Civic.

Rhonda moves his drink away from him, out of
reach. He takes a vial of pills out of his
pocket.

EXT. LE VAUDEVILLE RESTAURANT - 1 HOUR LATER

American couples' table is empty. James, stoned
drunk, signs credit receipt, gives it to Waiter
#1, points to his left.

            JAMES
Garçon, what building is that ol'
building over there?
     (sings)
"Over there, over there..."

            WAITER #1
It is the Paris stock exchange,
known as the Bourse de Paris. And
did you know that "garçon" means
"boy?" Today we say "serveur"...
sir.

            JAMES
Yeah. Beautiful archac-tec... it
must be *very* ol', I betcha. Right?

                    WAITER #1
          Yes, sir. Quite. Will there be
          anything else this evening. Sir?

James points straight ahead, further down the
street, to an office building where lights
shine in many windows.

                    JAMES
          Yeah, what's that one? With the
          letters, the red AFP, on the top?

                    WAITER #1
          The Agence France-Presse building,
          monsieur. The news agency.

                    JAMES
          Noose? I was starin' at Emeril City
          all night. Izzit... izzit open?

Waiter #1 shrugs. He walks away with receipt,
eyes rolling.

The Goodrichs stand.

                    RHONDA
          Let's get our driver. I wanna go to
          the Latin Quarter.

                    JAMES
          Uno minuto, Charo. Let's check out
          this A-fap deal.

                    RHONDA
          Jim, we have two nights left, we'll
          go tomorrow. We had plans--

                    JAMES
          Plans, shmans. Come on.

James steps off the curb, stumbles.

                    JAMES (CONT'D)
          Follow me. Shh. Stop stecret stuff.
                         80

Rhonda and Ben look at each other.

James regains his footing. They walk down the empty street. A distant CAR BACKFIRES.

> JAMES (CONT'D)
> Gum shots. Rum for your life!

James hustles Rhonda and Ben down the street.

INT. MAIN LOBBY, AFP BUILDING - MINUTES LATER

James, out of breath, talks to SECURITY GUARD, who sits in glass enclosed booth. Security Guard picks up phone.

Rhonda and Ben, out of breath, wait by front door.

NEWS CLERK emerges from door on first floor landing.

> NEWS CLERK
> You want to talk to the police
> about the car crash?

> JAMES
> Yes, por favor, we do. We, not that
> oui, we don't speak French, we, um--

> NEWS CLERK
> I see. Well, there are no police
> here tonight. I am very new here,
> too, as it happens, so... can you
> give me one quick minute, please?

News Clerk exits through door.

> RHONDA
> Jim, that was a car backfiring.

                    JAMES
          It was a gung. Okay, I know what
          gums sound like. Jesus.

                    BEN
          Dad, let's just go. And stop the
          stupid Spanish already.

News Clerk re-enters from door, AFP REPORTER #1
in tow.

                    AFP REPORTER #1
          Monsieur, madame, I can help you.
          We can file a report right now.

                    JAMES
               (to Rhonda, whispers)
          Don' mention cameras, don' talk
          about threats, just--

                    RHONDA
          Oh, really? I get it, Jimbo.

Ben yawns. He follows his parents up the
stairs.

INT. NEWSROOM, AFP BUILDING - MINUTES LATER

It's deserted. Empty desks, unmanned computer
monitors.

AFP Reporter #1 faces Rhonda and James at a
desk. AFP REPORTER #2 sits in front of computer
terminal.

Ben is fast asleep, stretched out on two
chairs.

                    AFP REPORTER #1
          Tell me what you saw.

                    JAMES
          Well, um, yeah, we, uh... hey Rhon,
          go 'head.

                    RHONDA
          James, lay down. That's a good boy.
          He's had a rough day. Okay, we got
          into a taxi at the Eiffel Tower--

INT. NEWSROOM - 1 HOUR LATER

News Clerk eavesdrops from hallway as AFP
Reporter #2 finishes typing.

AFP Reporter #1 is on the phone, writing on a
small pad.

INT. VARIOUS WORLDWIDE NEWSROOMS - MONTAGE -
DAY / NIGHT

Teletype machines spit out the Goodrichs' story
in newsrooms worldwide: Tokyo, New York,
London, Rome, Sydney, Paris...

INT. NEWSROOM, AFP BUILDING - SAME TIME - NIGHT

Ben still sleeps on the chairs. AFP Reporter #1
hangs up phone, gives piece of paper to James.

                    AFP REPORTER #1
          It is set. Tomorrow morning, ten-
          thirty sharp, ring this number.
          Police Officer Le Baron will be
          expecting your call... and tonight,
          madame, I have arranged for you my
          personal limousine driver.

News Clerk dashes down hallway, dialing a cell
number.

EXT. AFP BUILDING - SEVERAL MINUTES LATER

Beige limo speeds away.

Monique hides in bushes, watches limo depart.
She looks up at second floor window, sees News
Clerk smiling down at her.

She puts flip cell in her purse. Nearby lays
unconscious CHAUFFEUR, damp blue rag near his
nostrils.

INT. BEIGE LIMO - MINUTES LATER

PIERRE, late 20's, drives slowly. Goodrichs sit
in rear, Ben asleep on Rhonda's shoulder.

                    RHONDA
          I'm so glad we went on record.

                    JAMES
          Me too, babe.

EXT. REAR ENTRANCE, RITZ HOTEL - MINUTES LATER

Beige limo stops in front of revolving doors,
now cordoned off with yellow police tape.

INT. BEIGE LIMO - CONTINUOUS

Ben SNORES.

                    RHONDA
                  (whispers)
          The Ritz? That's weird.

                    JAMES
          Monsieur, this isn't our hotel.
          We're down the street, on the
          right. The Vérité.

Pierre turns around, his gun aimed at limo's roof.

>   PIERRE
>   It is good you did not tell them
>   you took pictures. One of my
>   brothers will see you in the
>   morning. One more chance, give him
>   the film. No word to police, no one
>   gets hurt. ¿Comprende?

>   JAMES
>   *Another* brother? What are you guys,
>   the fuckin' Karamazovs? Listen,
>   there *is* no film, it's been shipped
>   to the United States, so leave us
>   the fuck alone already. Kapish?

Ben opens his eyes, sees the gun, shuts them tight.

>   PIERRE
>   We shall see. Just get out!

INT. OFFICER LE BARON'S OFFICE - NEXT DAY - MORNING

>   TITLE OVER: MON., SEP. 1, 1997, 10:30 A.M.

OFFICER LE BARON, late 30's, sweats profusely, nervously smokes a cigarette. He wears name tag "Hercule Le Baron, Commissaire de Police."

Laurent, Monique, Rémy, Pierre surround him.

The phone RINGS. Monique points gun at Le Baron's head, motions for him to answer. On the third ring he does.

>   OFFICER LE BARON
>   Oui?

INT. RHONDA'S & JAMES'S ROOM - CONTINUOUS

Ben reads his Detective comic book in his room.
James is on the phone. Rhonda sits next to him.

>   JAMES
>   This is James Goodrich. Officer Le
>   Baron is expecting my call.
>   (beat)
>   Hello? I was told--

INT. OFFICER LE BARON'S OFFICE - CONTINUOUS

>   OFFICER LE BARON
>   There is no Le Baron here. Perhaps
>   if you call back at, say, fifteen-
>   hundred hours?
>   (beat, then quickly)
>   They say you have photos, guard
>   them, they may be the key--

INT. RHONDA'S & JAMES'S ROOM - CONTINUOUS

James hears a muffled GUNSHOT, followed by
INDISTINCT FRENCH CONVERSATION, then a CLICK.

He looks at phone, hangs it up.

>   RHONDA
>   Talk.

>   JAMES
>   They said to try back at three
>   o'clock, I think, and--

>   RHONDA
>   What?

>   JAMES
>   Unfrickin' believable.

                    BEN'S VOICE (O.C.)
        I told you something's fishy.

The phone RINGS. James jumps, picks it up.
Rhonda picks up an extension.

                    JAMES
        Yes?

INTERCUT: CONCIERGE & JAMES

A pissed off Jacques sits impatiently in nearby
chair.

                    CONCIERGE
        I have a message from your brother
        in New York. He says you're in all
        the papers and Mr. Willis' people
        are getting more excited about you.

                    JAMES
        Really? What else did he say?

                    CONCIERGE
        He said to keep doing what you're
        doing. Also, two messages from CNN
        marked urgent.
                (sotto voce)
        Monsieur, this paparazzi you fought
        with the other day? He is here now.
        He offered me money to ransack your
        room, of course I would never
        permit such a thing. He says you
        have something for him. He looks
        very angry.

                    JAMES
        Holy Christ. Um, gimme the CNN
        messages.
                (to Rhonda)
        Pen, pen, Rhonda. Quick.

She hangs up phone, finds a pen, gives it to
him.

                    RHONDA
What're we gonna do?

                    JAMES
One second, Rhon, wait a minute.
Okay, go.

James listens, writes a phone number on scrap
of paper, disconnects, dials new phone number.

Ben comes into their room.

                    CNN SECRETARY'S VOICE (V.O.)
CNN, Ken Jarrett's office.

                    JAMES
Hello, this is James Goodrich, I--

                    CNN SECRETARY'S VOICE (V.O.)
I'll connect you, Mr. Goodrich.

INTERCUT: JAMES & KEN JARRETT

                    KEN JARRETT
Jarrett here. By the way, you folks
related to *the* Goodrichs?

                    JAMES
Ken, you left me two urgent
messages. What's urgent?

                    KEN JARRETT
Mr. Goodrich, CNN is here to help.
You're smack dab in the middle of a
worldwide media event and you need
to be very careful who you talk to.
Do you get that?

                    JAMES
Beginning to, yeah. There's a bad
guy in my lobby right now.

James pours a drink from bar.

                            88

                    KEN JARRETT
          Stay in your room. An armed body
          guard from CNN, name is Richard
          Zimbalist. He's on his way to pick
          you up. Can you sit tight?

James looks at Rhonda.

                    JAMES
          Couldn't get much tighter.

                    KEN JARRETT
          Good. Wait for his call.

James hangs up phone. The phone RINGS back
immediately. He picks up the handset. He's
starting to enjoy this.

                    JAMES
          Jim Goodrich here.

                    RICHIE Z'S VOICE (V.O.)
          I got rid of that paparazzi slime
          ball, sir. Name is Richie Z, here
          to take you to CNN. Ready?

James downs the drink.

INT. LOBBY, CNN HEADQUARTERS - 30 MINUTES LATER
- DAY

RICHIE Z, 40's, muscular build, always wears a
trench coat, introduces the Goodrichs to ROB
FELDMAN, 50's, tough-talking yet gentle
newsman, shades of Lou Grant.

                    RICHIE Z
               (to the Goodrichs)
          This is Rob Feldman, CNN producer.

Richie Z takes a lobby seat.

FELDMAN
A pleasure. Come on, let's get you
guys up to my office. Can I get you
something to eat or drink?

Rhonda, James, Ben follow Feldman to elevator.

JAMES
(considers)
Drink?

Rhonda sighs.

INT. FELDMAN'S OFFICE - MINUTES LATER

Ten TV monitors tuned to different TV networks
worldwide, all reporting the Princess Diana
story.

The Goodrichs sit near Feldman. He's on the
phone.

FELDMAN
Yes, they're the American witnesses
to the Diana crash... yes, they're
leaving tomorrow... yep, uh huh...
okay, you know where to find me.

Feldman shakes his head, hangs up. Ben leafs
through his Detective comic book nonchalantly.

FELDMAN (CONT'D)
Can you believe these bozos?

RHONDA
What'd they say?

FELDMAN
Not much. Said the police chief
will call back in an hour. Bozos, I
swear to--

                    BEN
              (not looking up)
          I'm not surprised.

                    FELDMAN
          Why is that, son?

                    BEN
          I don't know. Those police are like
          really weird. Like the night of the
          crash, in the tunnel, they just...
          they just stood there doing
          nothing, like they were--

          JAMES   BEN
     Ben, that's enough.   And I keep seeing
                              this creepy lady
                              everywhere. And
                              everybody wants my
                              Dad's film, the--

                    RHONDA
          Ben!

     James looks at Ben incredulously. Beat.

                    FELDMAN
          You have photos?

                    JAMES
          No. Ben, put the comic book away.
          Very vivid imagination.

                    FELDMAN
          Goodrichs, you've stumbled into the
          biggest story since JFK, you've got
          an *American* perspective that--

     Feldman's INTERCOM BUZZES.

                    FELDMAN (CONT'D)
          You guys ready to tell your story?
          We're live in five. Good to go?

Rhonda and James exchange looks. Rhonda shrugs.
James gives Feldman a nod.

Rhonda looks at herself in wall mirror, reaches
for her lip gloss. James looks at his
reflection in glass picture frame, fixes his
hair.

> FELDMAN (CONT'D)
> Okay, great. Now, right after the
> interview we'll drive you back to
> your hotel. You'll freshen up, then
> you'll luncheon at the Jules Verne
> Room, top of the Eiffel, CNN table,
> incredible view, best cuisine in
> Paris, order whatever you want, a
> fine bottle of French wine, try to
> relax, our treat, of course. Then
> you'll come back here. We'd like to
> book you on Larry King tonight.

Rhonda and James exchange glances. James nods.

Feldman lights a cigar, blows a smoke ring. He
picks up RINGING phone, listens, winks at them.

> FELDMAN (CONT'D)
> They're ready for their close-ups.

Feldman hangs up phone. WALTER RODGERS, late
60's, a sharply dressed seasoned newsman,
appears in doorway.

He signals the Goodrichs to follow him. They do
so.

Feldman presses a button, door shuts
automatically.

> FELDMAN (CONT'D)
> (into intercom)
> Judy, get me CNN Europe... and tell
> Richie Z to make sure they have
> their passports... hi Peter, Rob

Feldman here. Listen, something's
rotten in the state of France, man,
and I ain't talkin' about no Brie.

Feldman blows another smoke ring.

INT. SMALL FRONT PARLOR, GOODRICH SUITE - 1
HOUR LATER

Ben unlocks the door, Rhonda and James follow
him inside. Lots of message notes on the floor
near the door. Ben hands them to James, who
reads each one, passing them to Rhonda.

          JAMES
Urgent from the Beeb, German TV,
Washington Post, the Today Show,
the New York Times...? Whoa, CBS,
AB... holy crap, I gotta call
David, this is--

          RHONDA
No. No time now, Richie's waiting
for us outside. Lemme grab the--

Rhonda hurries to wall safe, removes passports.

          BEN
Dad, are we famous?

          JAMES
Soon, little man. Very soon.
    (to Rhonda)
Gimme five minutes, Rhon. I have to
talk to him right now.
    (to himself, giddy)
This is just what the doctor
ordered. Getting Diana'd!

INT. JULES VERNE ROOM, EIFFEL TOWER - LATER -
AFTERNOON

Lunch is almost finished. WAITER #2 refills
wine glasses. MAITRE D' approaches table.

                    MAITRE D'
          Monsieur, excusez-moi, but there is
          an urgent long distance for you.

          RHONDA   BEN
     I never heard so many   Bet it's Uncle Dave.
     urgents.

                    JAMES
          Bet you're right.

                    MAITRE D'
          If you will follow me?

Two PHOTOGRAPHERS, passing by their table, snap
a couple photos.

James stands up, follows Maitre D' to private
phone. James picks it up.

                    JAMES
          Good news about cousin Brucey?

                    MINDY STEVENS' VOICE (V.O.)
          It's Mindy Stevens, James. I'm a
          producer with Larry King Live in
          Washington. How're you holding up?

                    JAMES
          Tell you what, Mindy. My head is
          spinning.

INTERCUT: JAMES & MINDY STEVENS

                    MINDY STEVENS
          Well, I won't keep you. I'm just
          confirming your 3 A.M. on-air.

                    JAMES
          That's a *definite*? Oh, I thought--

          MINDY STEVENS
Absolutely, you're a big part of
this story. We'll be airing in New
York at 9 P.M. Eastern. Larry wants
you and your wife for the whole
hour. I know it'll be very late in
Paris but is that doable?

          JAMES
Okay. So, what's the next step?

          MINDY STEVENS
We'll call your hotel room at
midnight for the pre-interview. At
2 A.M. you'll be picked up by limo
to drive you to the studio. Doable?

          JAMES
Yes. Indeedly doable.

          MINDY STEVENS
Excellent, we'll speak to you then.
Oh, and James? I know you've been
through a lot here. We'll make this
as painless as possible, I promise.

He hangs up the phone.

          JAMES
       (to himself)
Painless. Definitely doable.

He trots back to his family's table. Giddy.

          JAMES (CONT'D)
We're gonna be on Larry King
tonight, kids. Done deal.
       (to Waiter #2)
Wine list, garçon? Oh, and a double
Perrier on the rocks, for Junior
here.

Rhonda and Ben exchange uneasy glances.

EXT. CATWALK, JULES VERNE ROOM - LATER

Ben looks at Paris skyline through coin-op viewer.

Rhonda and James stroll the landing, arm-in-arm. A tear rolls down her cheek. She tries to hide it but he wipes it away.

> JAMES
> You okay, babe?

> RHONDA
> (overwhelmed)
> Paris is so beautiful. I mean, my God, look at us, we're in *Paris*. For a moment I allowed myself to forget what happened, and then... boom! Reality hits and I--

> JAMES
> I know just what you mean, babe.

> RHONDA
> No, you don't know "just what I mean, babe." You don't have a fucking clue, you have stars in your eyes. The booze has taken you over and I don't even know who you are anymore.

James steps angrily away. Ben overhears them.

> JAMES
> Where the hell did that come from?

> RHONDA
> (whispers)
> Keep your voice down.

> JAMES
> Lemme tell you something. When you were an actress you would've killed for attention like this. I know

that and so do you, so gimme a
freakin' break, okay, cut me some
slack here. Don't tell me about
"stars in my eyes" bullshit because
that's a bunch of crap.

Rhonda looks directly into James's eyes, shakes
her head.

> JAMES (CONT'D)
> You know what you are? You're a
> freaking buzz kill bitch.

Rhonda pulls herself together, puts on her
Chanel sunglasses, decidedly walks away towards
Ben.

James kicks the wall.

INT. FELDMAN'S OFFICE - HOUR LATER

Guilt-stricken James and dispirited Ben sit in
an office corner, watching the non-stop
Princess Diana coverage. Rhonda sits away from
them, near Feldman's desk.

Feldman speaks into the phone.

A clock displays 3:45 P.M.

> FELDMAN
> The Goodrichs have been trying
> to... well, here's the scoop.
> Either you depose them today or
> watch CNN tonight. We have no
> problem letting the world know how
> your police force is mishandling
> this entire investigation.

James and Ben join Rhonda at Feldman's desk.
Feldman listens a moment longer, then hangs up
phone.

                    FELDMAN (CONT'D)
               (to himself)
          Six? Bungling bunch of bozos.
               (to the Goodrichs)
          The police will depose you at six.

EXT. BRIGADE CRIMINELLE BUILDING - EARLY
EVENING

It's cloudy, it's chilly, it's drizzling.
Richie Z hustles Goodrichs out of CNN van.

REPORTERS, CAMERAMEN, satellite dishes are
behind a roped-off area across the street. The
Goodrich family is their focus.

Richie Z escorts Goodrichs up the front steps.
Guard #1 and GUARD #2, holding rifles, block
the entrance. Richie Z shows his ID card. Guard
#1 opens one of the sizable doors.

Guard #2 signals inside to FRENCH POLICEMAN #2
and FRENCH POLICEMAN #3.

                    RICHIE Z
               (to Rhonda, James, Ben)
          It's okay. Go in.

They enter. Guard #1 shuts the door. CLANG.

INT. MAIN LOBBY, NEAR STAIRWELL - CONTINUOUS

Rhonda jumps at the CLANG.

The Goodrichs and Richie Z follow French
Policeman #2, French Policeman #3 across lobby
to dimly lit doorway at stairwell entrance.

                    BEN
          Creepsylvania.

INT. SIXTH FLOOR POLICE AREA - MINUTES LATER

They enter from stairwell door.

Darkly lit, cement walls, wooden benches. Dingy and smoky.

French Policeman #2 approaches FRENCH POLICEMAN #4, who mans a security booth. They confer.

French Policeman #2, French Policeman #3 exit via the stairwell door.

> FRENCH POLICEMAN #4
> (in French, to James)
> We need your passports, please.

> RICHIE Z
> (to James)
> He wants your passports.
> (in French)
> They don't understand French.

Rhonda gives the three passports to French Policeman #4, who hastily scrutinizes each one in turn.

> FRENCH POLICEMAN #4
> (in French, to Richie Z)
> You must wait outside the building.

> RICHIE Z
> (in French)
> I was told I could wait in here.

> FRENCH POLICEMAN #4
> (in French)
> No, monsieur. That is incorrect.

> RHONDA
> What's going on, Richie?

                    RICHIE Z
          They want me to leave. Don't you
          worry, Rhonda, you have my card,
          call me soon as you're done. I'll
          be waiting in the van. It's okay.

Rhonda hugs Richie Z. He exits via the
stairwell door.

The Goodrichs walk further into police area,
bustling with a lot of POLICEMEN activity.

Gerard Barbette, wearing Givenchy suit, enters
from his office. He is 180 degrees from when we
first met him on page 2: now clean shaven,
well-tanned, confident.

He confers with French Policeman #4 at security
booth.

The Goodrichs sit on a musty bench in waiting
area. Barbette ambles his way over to them.

                    GERARD BARBETTE
          I am Gerard Barbette, Capitaine de
          Police, in charge of the Diana
          investigation. We have to wait for
          the, um, the... translator. As you
          see, my command of English, it is
          not, not so good, yes? Excusez-moi.

He laughs. The Goodrichs smile politely.
Barbette returns to his office, shuts door.

                    JAMES
                 (whispers)
          His English ain't really so bad.

Stairwell door opens a crack. It's Laurent. He
pushes a small blue hatbox inside. The DOOR
CREAKS as it closes shut.

                    RHONDA (V.O.)
          Spending my last night in Paris
          waiting for a translator. No time
          to go shopping. This sucks.

A wall clock displays 7:05 P.M.

FRENCH POLICEMAN #5 walks towards stairwell
door, picks up hatbox, places it on table near
security booth.

Barbette emerges from office, hands documents
to French Policeman #4. Barbette sees hatbox,
picks it up.

                    GERARD BARBETTE
               (in French, to himself)
          Oh. I have been looking for this.

                    JAMES
          Officer? We've been here over an
          hour. Is the translator coming?

                    GERARD BARBETTE
          He is still stuck in the traffic.

                    JAMES
          Stuck in...? How much longer?

                    GERARD BARBETTE
          Soon, I think, but I cannot say for
          certain. You are free to leave.

                    JAMES
          Leave? Why would we leave?

                                   DISSOLVE TO:

The clock displays 7:25 P.M.

INTERPRETER, mid 40's, painfully skinny, enters
from stairwell door. He wears an ill-fitting
suit and an unlit cigarette stub dangles from
his mouth. He wheezes.

He confers with French Policeman #4, who presses a buzzer.

MARIE TIESSART, mid 30's, pretty policewoman, enters from another office. She joins Interpreter.

They approach the Goodrichs.

                    INTERPRETER
I am the Interpreter, sorry to be a little bit late. This is Inspecteur Marie Tiessart. She will take your deception tonight.

Interpreter glances at pocket watch.

                INTERPRETER (CONT'D)
I do not have much time. So! Good Inspecteur, if you please?

Ben covertly mouths the word "deception" to Rhonda and James.

Marie Tiessart leads them into Barbette's office.

INT. GERARD BARBETTE'S OFFICE - LATER - TWILIGHT

The hands of a wall clock display 8:15 P.M.

Marie Tiessart sits at computer keyboard. The rest of them sit around a large paper-cluttered wooden table.

Barbette turns away, opens hatbox, peeks inside. He takes out hand-written note that says "*Merci!*" He's clearly puzzled.

                    MARIE TIESSART
            (in French)
        ...and when you spotted the body of
        Princess Diana, please describe
        exactly what you saw.

                    INTERPRETER
        So, Monsieur Goodrich, the good
        Inspecteur, she wants to know, the
        Princess, did she appear to be
        alive or dead when you saw her?

                    JAMES
        I didn't see her.

                    INTERPRETER
        Ahhh, you are changing your story,
        then, no?

                    RHONDA
        I saw her.

                    INTERPRETER
        Then *you* answer the question.

                    JAMES
        Shouldn't she answer the question
        when you take *her* deposition?

                    INTERPRETER
        It is late. They decide to take
        just one decep... um, *deposition*.

He smiles knowingly at Ben.

                    INTERPRETER (CONT'D)
        They will combine the answers.

                    RHONDA
        Fine.

                    JAMES
        No, it is *not* fine. This isn't how--

                    INTERPRETER
You are in a rush so we have just
one. We do it this way. Good
Inspecteur, you may continue.

                                DISSOLVE TO:

The clock displays 9:03 P.M. Interpreter claps
hands twice.

                    INTERPRETER (CONT'D)
We are done here. La fin.

Marie Tiessart presses keyboard button. A
document emerges from printer.

Interpreter staples it, indicates signature
line to James.

                    INTERPRETER (CONT'D)
You will sign here.

                    JAMES
You're kidding, right? You know I
don't read French.

                    INTERPRETER
It is okay. I am the interpreter,
so of course I can see what is
written. I will read it to you,
then you sign it. Yes?

James hesitates. He looks at Rhonda.

                    RHONDA
Sign it. I wanna get out of here.

                    BEN
Yeah dad, please. Just sign it.

                    JAMES
How can I sign it? I can't read it.

                    INTERPRETER
          Sorry you do not trust--

                    JAMES
          It has nothing to do with... look,
          you have my statement, we've done
          our duty. Call Richie Z, let's go.
               (on second thought, to
               Barbette)
          Um, can I, can I get a copy of
          that? For my lawyer to see? And
          then maybe I could sign it and--

                    BARBETTE
          That would be a waste of time. We
          cannot use this as evidence unless
          we get your signature right now.

                    JAMES (V.O.)
          Shit. I need proof we were here.

The tension in the room is palpable.

The Goodrichs stand up, walk towards the closed
exit door. James stops in his tracks.

                    JAMES
          One sec. Can I maybe get a quick
          photo of the three of you, with
          Benjy? You know, for my photo album
          kind of thing?

James takes out his camera. Barbette shrugs his
approval. He poses next to Marie Tiessart and
Interpreter.

James pushes a reluctant Ben into frame,
quickly snapping a photo of the foursome.

                    JAMES (CONT'D)
          That's great. Thank you.

GERARD BARBETTE
De rien, you are welcome. And
because of the long wait, for your
son, may I present a gift?

Barbette opens hatbox, removes Paris police cap
with police badge affixed.

He gives cap to Ben, who puts it on his head,
backward. Barbette chuckles as he turns the cap
around.

GERARD BARBETTE (CONT'D)
No no, Ben, no. You wear it like
this. For respect.

Ben turns cap around, backward.

BEN
But I like to wear it like *this*.

GERARD BARBETTE
Okay, okay. I give up.
(to Ben, confidentially)
Listen, this badge is real and that
cap is one of a kind. Now you will
always remember your visit to
Paris. Yes?

BEN (V.O.)
How could I ever forget it?

Ben nods and smiles at Barbette, then holds
Paris police badge directly towards camera.

BEN
Dad, take another picture *now*.

James doesn't miss a beat. He snaps another
photo.

                    GERARD BARBETTE
              (quickly, out of nowhere)
          Benjy, did your daddy take pictures
          in the tunnel?

                    BEN
          We--

                    JAMES
          I had the camera in the tunnel.

Barbette stares at James. James stares back.

                    GERARD BARBETTE
          Monsieur, did you take photos in
          the tunnel two nights ago? Yes or
          no?

James gives Barbette a long, hard look.

                    JAMES
          Only paparazzi would take photos of
          a car crash. I'm not a paparazzo.
              (beat, smiles)
          Au revoir, mi amigos.

The Goodrichs exit.

Barbette glances uncertainly at Marie Tiessart
and Interpreter.

INT. CNN VAN - MINUTES LATER - NIGHT

Richie Z drives the Goodrichs. Ben looks out
van window.

                    RHONDA
          Bunch of Keystone Kops, I swear.

                    JAMES
          How 'bout Inspector Clousseau?
              (imitates Interpreter)
          "So sorry you do not trust me..."

                    BEN
        Hey dad, what's a beau-zo? Is that
        like French for dim-wit?
                (in a poor French accent)
        Oh man, I could really go for zum
        French fries and zum cheeseburgers.
        Richie Z, can you make zat happen?

Richie Z steers a hard right into McDonald's
parking lot.

                    RICHIE Z
        Roger that, Moan-swah Benny G.

INT. CONCIERGE DESK - 30 MINUTES LATER

Rhonda and Ben approach Concierge. James
carries the food.

                    RHONDA
        Don't put any calls through
        tonight, please. I'm exhausted.

                    JAMES
                (ignores Rhonda)
        François, I'm expecting a VIP call
        from CNN at twelve mid, we'll need
        a wake-up call tomorrow morning at
        eight A. Is that doable?

                    CONCIERGE
        Got it, yes, consider it done. And
        here are today's messages for you.

Concierge motions his head while giving James
message notes.

                    CONCIERGE (CONT'D)
                (whispers)
        There are many reporters in that
        room. Some have been waiting hours.

Rhonda and James exchange looks.

                    BRITISH REPORTER'S VOICE (O.S.)
        Mr. Goodrich? Mrs. Goodrich?

The Goodrichs see an onslaught of REPORTERS,
SOUNDMEN, TV CAMERAMEN approaching them.

          BRITISH REPORTER   GERMAN REPORTER
        May we have an   Mr. Goodrich, do you
        exclusive interview?   have a few minutes?

          ITALIAN REPORTER   FRENCH REPORTER
        We have a few   Monsieur, madame, may
        questions for you.   I introduce myself?

                        RHONDA
        Wait, wait. Everybody. Please stop!

Complete silence.

                        RHONDA (CONT'D)
        It's enough. No more interviews. We
        are done here. La fin.

                        BRITISH REPORTER
        We promise to leave you alone after
        this. I've been waiting to see you
        all day. You *must* share your story
        with the world. This is Princess
        Diana we're talking about. For
        goodness' sake. For the Princess'
        sake.

James considers. He looks at Rhonda, who shakes
her head.

                        JAMES
                (turns away from Rhonda)
        Okay. Let's go, everybody. In here.

James walks into anteroom. Rhonda fumes, but
she and Ben follow him. Reporters, Soundmen,
Cameramen follow.

                    BEN
        Gimme my food, dad. I'm goin'
        arriba arriba.

                    JAMES
        No you're not. You're staying here.

                    RHONDA
            (whispers, to James)
        I'll talk to you about this later.

                    JAMES
        Talk to me about what?

INT. RHONDA'S & JAMES'S ROOM - 1 HOUR LATER -
NIGHT

The room is dark. Rhonda and James, fully
dressed, lay on top of the bed's blankets.
Rhonda can't sleep. James snores.

The phone on her night table RINGS. She nudges
him awake, turns on lamp. A nearby clock
displays 11:57 P.M.

                    RHONDA
        I'm not doing that fucking Larry
        King show.

She ignores the RINGING phone, pulls blankets
over her head. James reaches past her upper
body to grab phone. He accidentally smacks her
head.

                    RHONDA (CONT'D)
        Ow! Answer it, glory hound.

She throws a blanket off the bed, smacks his
shoulder hard.

                    JAMES
        Ow! I'm trying to. I didn't see
        you.

He grabs the phone handset, turns on his night table lamp. He rubs his shoulder, glares at her.

                    JAMES (CONT'D)
          Hello, James Goodrich speaking.

                    JUDY LYONS' VOICE (V.O.)
               (no nonsense)
          Hi. Judy Lyons, segment producer.
          Did we wake you?

                    JAMES
          Yes, absolutely. I mean... wait,
          hold on? Lemme get... one, one sec.

James covers phone's mouthpiece and pushes Rhonda, gesturing for her to pick up the desk phone extension.

She elbows him in the ribs, gets out of bed. James represses his new pain. A pissed-off Rhonda picks up desk phone.

                    JAMES (CONT'D)
          Say hi, Rhonda.

                    RHONDA
          Hello.

Uncomfortable beat.

                    JUDY LYONS' VOICE (V.O.)
          Okay! On the line with us is Mr.
          Andrew Gates from Time magazine.

                    ANDREW'S VOICE (V.O.)
          Hi Rhonda, hi James.

                    JAMES
          Hi.

Uncomfortable beat.

JUDY LYONS' VOICE (V.O.)
Great. James, let's start with you.
What's the first thing you remember
about the crash?

JAMES
Well, we were in a taxi and about
to enter this tunnel. I saw blue
flashing lights up ahead and--

RHONDA
Sweetheart, excuse me, but you
didn't see blue flashing lights
when we were outside the tunnel.

JAMES
Hon, please don't tell me what I
saw or didn't see. Anyway--

RHONDA
Well, I didn't see the lights until
we got further *inside* the tunnel.

JAMES
May I continue? Please? Again, I
saw the *reflection* of lights on the
tunnel wall as we approached the
tunnel. Did I say that correctly,
Rhon? Judy, you clear on that?

JUDY LYONS' VOICE (V.O.)
Okay folks, take a deep breath,
it's late, you're both stressed.
Rhonda, tell me what you saw.

RHONDA
Well, we got into a taxi near the
Eiffel Tower, after what was
supposed to be a romantic cruise on
the River Seine--

JAMES
Are you kidding? I just told them
we were in the taxi. Why are you--

                    RHONDA
I think it's important we start
from the cruise and to talk about
how our cab driver--

                    JAMES
They don't care about our cabbie,
they wanna know about the crash.

          JUDY LYONS' VOICE (V.O.)
You know what? Rhonda, tell me
about when you saw Diana's body.

                    RHONDA
Well, before I saw her body, and of
course I didn't know it was *her*
body at the time. Anyway, I saw a
bunch of motorcycles, I saw
paparazzi. Oh, and I saw a
policeman who was--

                    JAMES
          (covers the mouthpiece)
There were *two* cops.

                    RHONDA
No, I saw one policeman inside the
tunnel. I didn't see the other two
until we got out--

          ANDREW'S VOICE (V.O.)
Hey folks, can I chime in?
          (beat)
Why not pull yourselves together
and, what say we pick you up a
half-hour early, at one-thirty, do
the pre-interview then. Make sense?

Rhonda hangs up the phone, and not softly.

                    JAMES
Perfecto.

                    113

James listens for a response, gets none, looks at phone, hangs it up. Rhonda walks back to bed, sits down next to him.

> JAMES (CONT'D)
> Well, you just so screwed that up.

> RHONDA
> What's wrong with you?

> JAMES
> What's wrong with...? Why didn't you just get to the point?

> RHONDA
> What part of not doing the show do you not understand?

> JAMES
> Shh, don't wake the Benster, let's get some sleep. I need another half-hour.

They turn off their lamps. James closes his eyes.

Rhonda sighs deeply, stares into the darkness. Sobs in silence. Her suppressed thoughts come to life.

EXT. REMY'S TAXI IN TUNNEL (EAST) - NIGHT (RHONDA'S FLASHBACK)

Taxi drives past black Mercedes. Rhonda looks at crash site through taxi's rear window. "Rapid Flash" bursts of light fluoresce the night. Princess Diana's body slumps over front passenger seat, on car's dashboard.

Diana's hair drapes down, obscures a clear view of her face.

INT. RHONDA'S & JAMES'S ROOM - 1 HOUR LATER

    TITLE OVER: TUE., SEP. 2, 1997, 1:15 A.M.

Phone RINGS. Rhonda startles awake.

James sleeps soundly. She shakes him, turns on
lamp, hands him the phone.

                    JAMES
               (groggy)
          Hello.

                    JUDY LYONS' VOICE (V.O.)
          Mr. Goodrich, it's Judy again.

                    JAMES
          Hi. We were--

                    JUDY LYONS' VOICE (V.O.)
          There's been a change in plans.

James sits up.

                    JAMES
          Okay. What's up?

                    JUDY LYONS' VOICE (V.O.)
          Well, it's the funniest thing. You
          know, for months we've been trying
          to snare Senator Bob Dole's wife
          Liddy on the show and, well,
          tonight we scored, she became
          available. Tonight only, can you
          believe that, James? Sorry for any
          bother but we're bumping your
          segment. Thanks--

                    JAMES
          Wait. What do you mean "bumping?"
          What does Libby Dole have to--

                    115

> JUDY LYONS' VOICE (V.O.)
> It's Liddy, not Libby. Thanks for
> your understanding, dear.
> (distracted)
> What? Oh! Okay, I gotta go. Bye.

The line disconnects. CLICK.

> JAMES
> Hello. Hellooooo?

He looks at handset, hangs up phone.

> JAMES (CONT'D)
> That bitch. She just hung up on me.

> RHONDA
> What happened?

> JAMES
> They bumped us.

> RHONDA
> Are you kidding me? I told you I
> didn't wanna do this.

> JAMES
> Well, guess what, Angel Breath, you
> got your wish 'cause you ain't
> doin' this.

> RHONDA
> Good. Go back to sleep.

> JAMES
> I can't believe this. *Bumped*?

> RHONDA
> Believe it, it's over. Thank God. I
> can't wait to go home tomorrow and
> put this behind me. Look at you,
> poor little actor boy. You should be
> used to getting bumped by now. Fame

116

is fleeting, honey. Time to grow up
and time to get a real job--

                    JAMES
          Would you shut the hell up already?

She pulls blankets over her head. James takes
flask out of his night table drawer, takes a
quick nip.

                    JAMES (CONT'D)
          I've really had it with your crap.

He walks out of room with flask, towards Ben's
room.

INT. BEN'S BEDROOM - CONTINUOUS

James looks lovingly down at Ben's bed. It's
empty!

He searches room in panic, opens suite door,
looks up and down hallway. No Ben in sight.

A toilet FLUSHES. Ben, oblivious to James, gets
back into bed. He pulls blankets over his head.

James sighs, looks at desk phone, sits in desk
chair, cranes his neck to see if Rhonda is in
view. She isn't. Good!

He picks up handset, dials a phone number,
listens.

                    ANSWERING MACHINE VOICE (V.O.)
          You have sixty-six new messages.

He sits up straighter.

                    ANSWERING MACHINE VOICE (V.O.)
          First new message:

>   LISA'S VOICE (V.O.)
>   Rhonda, it's Lisa, hi! The minute I
>   heard about Diana I wasn't
>   surprised you were in the middle of
>   it. Oh my God. Call me as soon as
>   you get home. And you looked so
>   great on TV, girlfrien', even
>   through the tears. Home safe.

James smiles slightly, shakes his head, presses
a button.

>   ANSWERING MACHINE VOICE (V.O.)
>   Message saved. Next new message:

>   MJ'S VOICE (V.O.)
>   Hi, this is for Rhonda and James
>   Goodrich. It's MJ from Good Morning
>   America. What a terrible tragedy
>   you witnessed, oh my goodness, I
>   can't even imagine. Anyway, it's
>   Joan Lunden's last week here at GMA
>   and she really wants an interview
>   with you. Please call me asap at
>   212-755-3--

His smile grows. He presses a button.

>   ANSWERING MACHINE VOICE (V.O.)
>   Message saved. Next new message:

>   PATRICK'S VOICE   RHONDA'S VOICE
>   (V.O.)   (O.S.)
>   This is Geraldo's   Jim, you coming to
>   office in New York.   bed or not?
>   He--

He hangs up phone, shit-eating grin on his
face.

>   JAMES
>   Be right there... "girlfrien'."
>   (to himself)
>   Libby Dole my ass. Bumped bullshit.

EXT. FRONT ENTRANCE, HOTEL VERITE - LATE
MORNING

Richie Z packs last of the luggage into CNN
van's trunk.

          RICHIE Z
    So Larry gave you the hook last
    night, huh?

          JAMES
    No, Richie, it was the other way
    around. We both decided not to--

          RHONDA
    Guys, excuse me. Five minutes. Be
    right back.

She walks across street. She's on a mission.
James and Ben look at each other. They follow
her.

INT. MAIN LOBBY, RITZ HOTEL - MINUTES LATER

Rhonda is at the front desk, adjacent to
crowded lobby. James and Ben stand beside her
as she speaks to DESK CLERK.

          DESK CLERK
    Can I be of service, madame?

          RHONDA
    A pen and paper, s'il vous plait?

James looks at her quizzically.

          RHONDA (CONT'D)
      (to James)
    I want to leave a note for Mohammed
    Al Fayed. He owns this hotel and my
    heart breaks for the loss of his
    son, I can't even imagine what--

Desk Clerk hands Rhonda a pen, a piece of Ritz
stationery, an envelope. She reaches for pen.

James puts his hand on top of hers, looks
directly into her eyes. Her true soul.

                    JAMES
          Leave it, honey. Leave it alone.

                    RHONDA
          But I wanted to--

                    JAMES
          I know. But it's enough. Like you
          said. It's time to go home.
               (to Desk Clerk)
          Thanks, monsieur.

James ushers Rhonda and Ben to front exit door.
On the way he sees three very familiar faces
sitting at a table.

                    JAMES (CONT'D)
               (to Rhonda and Ben)
          Hey! Meet you guys at the van.
          Gimme two minutes. Bathroom.

Rhonda nods. She and Ben hold hands as they
exit.

Jacques, Rémy, Pierre sit together. James walks
closer to sneak a better look. They spot him.

                    PIERRE
          Ah, look who is here! Good morning,
          my American friend. Just talking
          about you. You've met my brothers
          Jacques and Rémy, no doubt? Care to
          join us for a coffee?

They laugh.

                    RÉMY
               (whispers)
     Our oldest brother, our *step-*
     brother, is working today. And you
     know him, by the way. He's the bad
     guy, wrong side of the law and all
     that. That's how it goes, right?
     What can you do?
               (laughs)
     One lump or two, monsieur?

                    JAMES
               (grabs his crotch)
     Lump this.

They laugh louder. James walks to front exit
door.

                    RÉMY
     See you in New York, crazy frog.

James turns around, takes one more look at
them.

Jacques makes a gun out of forefinger and
thumb, aims it at James, shoots the "trigger,"
blows off the "gunsmoke."

                    JACQUES
     Bang bang, Monsieur Goody. I owe
     you a lump. Maybe two.

Jacques mimes a hard punch to his own jaw.

                    JACQUES (CONT'D)
     Oh, and you know what else? We know
     where you live. Have a nice flight!

They laugh hysterically as James exits.

END OF ACT II.

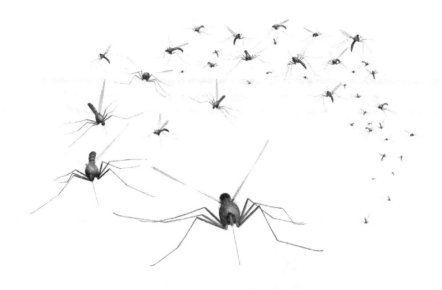

ACT THREE

September 1997

New York

INT. AIRPLANE, FIRST CLASS - 7 HOURS LATER -
DAY

A "DING" in the main cabin. PASSENGERS stand up.

                    PILOT'S VOICE (V.O.)
          Thanks for flying with us, folks.
          Welcome to New York and have an
          awesome day.

Rhonda and James retrieve carry-on luggage from
overhead bin. Ben stands in aisle, a few rows
in front of them.

                    RHONDA
          Go ahead, we're right behind you.

                    JAMES
          I swear, if I never live to see
          France again it won't be too soon.

                    RHONDA
          I think you mean it will be. Too
          soon.

Ben is fourth in line to depart the plane.

An entourage of NINE RED JACKET flight
attendants approach him. RED JACKET #1, a
heavyset black woman, leads the charge.

                    RED JACKET #1
          Are you Benjamin Goodrich, son?

Ben nods. Rhonda weaves her way down the
crowded aisle.

                    RHONDA
          I'm his mother. Is everything okay?

                    RED JACKET #1
          Everything's under control. We're
          just here to escort your family out
          of the gate.

Rhonda looks back at James.

INT. MAIN TERMINAL, JFK AIRPORT - MINUTES LATER

The Goodrichs follow Red Jacket #1. Nine Red
Jackets follow them. Rhonda groans.

                    JAMES
          Deep breath, honey. Try to calm
          down, babe.
                    (to Red Jacket #1)
          How'd the press even know we were
          on this flight?

                    RED JACKET #1
          Mr. Goodrich, you'd be surprised at
          what flashing a Ben Frank in front
          of a ticket agent can do. Even I
          have to admit, it is shameful.

Rhonda stops dead in her tracks. Everybody
follows suit.

                    RHONDA
          Can't believe this followed us
          home. Cannot believe it.

                    JAMES
          I can.
                    (confidentially)
          I checked the machine last night.
          Sixty-six messages.

                    RHONDA
          Why didn't you tell me?

                    JAMES
        Tell you? So I could hear that
        "glory hound" crap from you?

                    RED JACKET #1
                    (to Rhonda)
        Listen dear, we got a news tip from
        NBC that your house is surrounded
        by media trucks, so here's what I
        suggest. Do the interview now and--

                    RHONDA
        But we gave interviews, how many--

                    RED JACKET #1
        Not to America, you didn't. Do it
        now, sugar. Then it'll all be over.

Red Jacket #1 smiles, nods encouragingly.

INT. NEAR ROPED-OFF AREA, MAIN TERMINAL -
MINUTES LATER

Dozens of PASSENGERS surround roped-off area.
Some Passengers take photos of the Goodrichs.

Suzy Q, David, and an EAGER MALE PASSENGER
approach James.

                    EAGER MALE PASSENGER
        Can I get your autograph?

        DAVID GOODRICH   JAMES
        Buddy, can't you see   David, what the hell
        he's in crisis mode   are you doing here?
        here?   Suzy Q, my darlin'!

                    BEN
        Uncle Dave! Suzy!

The Goodrichs embrace Suzy Q and David.

Eager Male Passenger watches the family hugs.
He gives up his quest, walks away.

Rhonda, James, Ben, Suzy Q, David, Red Jacket
#1, Nine Red Jackets approach roped-off area.

Ben enjoys the attention.

> BEN (CONT'D)
> I guess they think we're
> celebrities now, Uncle Dave?

> SUZY Q
> You are! You guys rock.

> RED JACKET #1
> (to Nine Red Jackets)
> Keep an eye on them. Be right back.

Red Jacket #1 walks away.

INT. AWAY FROM ROPED-OFF AREA - CONTINUOUS

She surveys the area. Nobody's watching her.
She removes a $100 bill from underneath her
bra, kisses it, looks skyward.

> RED JACKET #1
> Thank you, dear Lordy baby Jesus!

INT. IN ROPED-OFF AREA - MOMENTS LATER

Red Jacket #1 rejoins gathering. The Goodrichs
are surrounded by TV REPORTERS, PHOTOGRAPHERS,
NEWSPAPER REPORTERS.

Several Passengers watch the Goodrichs being
interviewed.

Bursts of light from the camera flashes are
incessant.

INT. BLACK MERCEDES - 1 HOUR LATER

AMERICAN LIMO DRIVER #2 drives a black Mercedes limo. Rhonda, James, Ben, David and Suzy Q sit in back.

                    BEN
          The kids at school won't believe
          this whole thing.

David sniffs deeply a couple times.

                    RHONDA
          I hope she wasn't lying. No more
          interviews. Please!

                    DAVID GOODRICH
          Are you kidding? That's exactly
          what Jimbro needs. It's like...
          divine intervention or something,
          deus ex machina. Oh, here ya go.

David gives James a Fedex envelope.

                    JAMES
          Yeah, good. Thanks. So talk.

James rips open the Fedex. He pockets the film roll.

                    DAVID GOODRICH
          Well, I got me some good news, and
          I got me some caveat.

                    JAMES
          Okay. What does that mean?

                    DAVID GOODRICH
              (clears his throat)
          Okay.
              (beat, then oversells it)
          What you got goin' on now is free
          press, baby. F-R-double-E press.

David softly punches an unenthusiastic James's upper arm.

> JAMES
> Yeah, okay. Define that.

> DAVID GOODRICH
> (dramatic beat)
> You got the part.

Suzy Q tenses up.

Rhonda and Ben cheer wildly. James ecstatically punches David's upper arm several times. Very hard.

JAMES	DAVID GOODRICH
Yes, yes, yes! I knew it! Yeah! David, you rock!	Ow, that hurts. Really! Ow. Hold the applause. Ow!

SILENCE. David rubs his upper arm with a grimace. They wait for him to continue.

> DAVID GOODRICH (CONT'D)
> I said "got" the part. Caveat. Past tense. They called yesterday to renege. Not my fault, not my fault!

JAMES	SUZY Q
(mortified)	For the moment, for
What? Why?	the moment.

> DAVID GOODRICH (CONT'D)
> They said right now you're too well known, that it would look like stunt casting, and what they wanted was an unknown. Like you. Like you were. But they love ya, Jimbro, they really, really do. Really *did*.

> JAMES
> You can't put love in the bank, David. Shit. What am I gonna do? I can't believe this.

James holds his head in his hands.

                    RHONDA
          I can.

                    DAVID GOODRICH
               (beat, breaks the tension)
          Wow, it's just so great to see you
          guys! Hey Rhonda, you looked dyno
          on TV, babe, you know, you should
          def get back in the biz--

                    JAMES
          I told you to shut up about that.

Tinted glass partition rolls down.

                    AMERICAN LIMO DRIVER #2
          Sorry to interrupt the family fun,
          folks, but I think you might wanna
          see this.

Rhonda, James, Ben, Suzy Q look out the window.

David hides behind Suzy Q, sneaks a quick hit
of coke.

                    RHONDA
          How dare they!

                    DAVID GOODRICH
          Can't believe you guys are in the
          middle of this. Crazy! Great way to
          score with the chicks, Benny.

David winks. Ben doesn't understand what he
means.

EXT. GOODRICH HOUSE - CONTINUOUS

The black Mercedes moves slowly down the
street.

Satellite dishes on trucks, swarms of
REPORTERS, SOUNDMEN, CAMERAMEN, PHOTOGRAPHERS
define a suburban media circus.

Police cars barricade street traffic. AMERICAN
POLICEMAN #1 is clearly in charge.

INT. BLACK MERCEDES - CONTINUOUS

The black Mercedes, slowly, approaches the
Goodrich's house.

                    RHONDA
          What the hell is this?

                    DAVID GOODRICH
          I tried to tell you.

                    RHONDA
          She lied to me. That airport bitch.

                    BEN
          Calm down, mom.

                    RHONDA
          Everybody! Stop telling me to calm--

RAPPING on windshield. Black Mercedes stops. American
Limo Driver #2 rolls down all the windows.

                    AMERICAN POLICEMAN #1
          This block is closed off, folks.

                    RHONDA
          Excuse me, that's my house and I
          want you to get rid of these
          people. They're trespassing. I was
          told they wouldn't be here. We--

                    AMERICAN POLICEMAN #1
          That's all very nice, ma'am, but
          there's nothing we can do. You're
          public figures now.

EXT. GOODRICH HOUSE - CONTINUOUS

Rhonda gets out of black Mercedes. The family follows suit. American Limo Driver #2 unloads luggage.

TEN TEENAGE FRIENDS encircle Ben. TWO TEENAGE GIRLS hold each of his arms and look at him with adoration.

Ben makes eye contact with David. David gives Ben another wink and a thumbs-up.

A plump FEMALE REPORTER and a stocky MALE PHOTOGRAPHER wait across the street. They each lean against a parked car.

Male Photographer cavalierly snaps photos of Rhonda and James. Rhonda runs over to him.

              RHONDA
      Could you stop with the pictures?
      Please? I beg of you.

            MALE PHOTOGRAPHER
      Just doing my job, ma'am.

            FEMALE REPORTER
      All I want is a quick five minute
      interview, ma'am. Then me and Mike
      are done, we do a Houdini, okay?

Rhonda storms away. James, David, Suzy Q approach Female Reporter and Male Photographer.

            FEMALE REPORTER (CONT'D)
        (to Rhonda, loudly)
      You know, honey, if you won't talk
      to me, I can write whatever I want.

Male Photographer snaps more photos. She runs back to him.

                    RHONDA
        Give me that camera! You can't take
        pictures here.

She grabs camera, to no avail. She crosses the
street again.

                    RHONDA (CONT'D)
        Up yours, both of you. James,
        handle this for me, for God's sake.

                    FEMALE REPORTER
        Mr. Goodrich, how about a quote?

                    RHONDA
              (from across the street)
        And I don't care what you write,
        okay? I don't care what pictures
        you take. Just spell my name right.
        Ha! And go screw each other! Ha!

                    DAVID GOODRICH
              (to Female Reporter)
        Looks like that went well.

                    JAMES
        A quote. Okay. You know, I read on
        the return flight what the word
        "paparazzi" means, and I quote: "a
        swarm of bothersome mosquitoes,
        annoying pests," end quote. David,
        handle this for me, for God's sake.

James suddenly stops in his tracks because he
"sees" an invisible mosquito on Male
Photographer's arm.

                    JAMES (CONT'D)
              (to Male Photographer)
        Wait, don't move. Aha! A skeeter!

With open palm, James smacks Male
Photographer's upper arm hard. James eyes the
invisible squashed mosquito on his palm.

JAMES (CONT'D)
Gotcha! I got the paparazzo fuck.

James "wipes" his hands on his trousers,
crosses the street.

Ben and his Teenage Friends enter the house.

DAVID GOODRICH
You know who that is, right? James
Goodrich, the *actor*. That's
Goodrich, spelled like the tires.
Here's a news tip. He's up for a
major role in the new Bruce Willis
flick.

David holds a tightly rolled up rubber-banded
$100 bill, flicks it into his palm, white
powder falls out. He removes rubber band, slips
the $100 bill to Female Reporter.

DAVID GOODRICH (CONT'D)
How many papers can we get this in?

David walks toward the house, discreetly
licking his palm.

INT. "GOOD MORNING AMERICA" STUDIO - DAYS LATER
- MORNING

TITLE OVER: 2 DAYS LATER

THEME MUSIC. JOAN LUNDEN finishes up the
Goodrich interview.

INT. HOTEL SUITE, NEW YORK CITY - HOURS LATER

A desk clock displays 11:40 A.M.

Rhonda and James, well-dressed in their GMA interview clothes, sit on opposite ends of a long couch.

She's conversing on the hotel phone, watching James. He's happily paging through People magazine.

> RHONDA
> I won't be home in time for Ben. Can you pick him up from school?... Lisa, thanks so much.

Rhonda has an epiphany.

> RHONDA (CONT'D)
> You know what, can I call you later?... yes... well, he scheduled People at noon, Time magazine at two, then... wait, I gotta go... okay... bye bye.

She hangs up phone, stares at him. He stops reading, doesn't look at her, stares straight ahead.

> JAMES
> What?

> RHONDA
> *What?* You really wanna know *what?* You talked me into all this insane interview bullshit, that's what. I did this for you and I feel used, okay? I'm done, bump me. I'm toast.

James puts People magazine on coffee table.

> JAMES
> What are you...? The reporter from People's gonna be here in fifteen--

Rhonda picks up phone handset, holds it out for him.

                    RHONDA
        I'll say it again. Cancel these now
        or I will. They're exploiting us
        and I'm sick and tired of rehashing
        the same story. Aren't you?
                (sarcastic laugh)
        Look who I'm asking. I don't wanna
        get Diana'd anymore, James. I want
        my life back!

He's bewildered. She hangs up phone, moves
closer to him.

                    RHONDA (CONT'D)
        Jamie, we've been back three days
        and we've had, what, three hundred
        calls from the media? Every time we
        do an interview they ask for thirty
        more. I'm about to crack.

                    JAMES
        But I gotta generate press, babe.
        David said--

                    RHONDA
        David's a fucking idiot. It's the
        wrong kind of press!

Rhonda glares at him. She stands up, walks away.

James says nothing. He stares ahead into empty
space.

                    RHONDA (CONT'D)
        How can you not see that? You
        already lost a movie over this.
        You're a news item, moron, a *news*
        item. I wanna go home, and I wanna
        go now--

                    JAMES
        "I wanna go home. I wanna go now."
        So go the fuck home, Dorothy, I'll
        call you a cab, okay?

                    RHONDA
          I hate you. I really--

                    JAMES
          It's all a fuckin' game, I have to
          play by the rules, do what's best
          for my career. Telling me to give
          up interviews with Time and People?
          What kind of actor would do that?

                    RHONDA
          Actor? That's what you think this
          is about? Oh Jesus, you're not only
          an alcoholic in denial, you're a
          pill popping delusional, Jim, and I
          think you need some serious help. I
          know you do.

                    JAMES
          But I'm doing this for you and Ben.

She shakes her head, laughs at him in pity.

                    JAMES (CONT'D)
          Alright, I'll cancel the damn
          interviews. Fucking bitch.

Rhonda slaps him in the face. He looks at her,
stung.

INT. MASTER BATHROOM, GOODRICH HOUSE - DAYS
LATER - MORNING

     TITLE OVER: 2 DAYS LATER

Rhonda gets out of the shower, puts on a robe,
wraps her hair in a towel. She looks at herself
in the mirror.

Radio plays Princess Diana version of CANDLE IN
THE WIND. Her eyes well-up.

EXT. GOODRICH HOUSE - MOMENTS LATER

A white van, emblazoned with the Celebrity Hotline TV show logo, parks in driveway.

STEVE BERNHARDT, 40, "chiseled features" TV reporter, carries bouquet of roses. He walks to front door, presses doorbell/speaker button. It RINGS.

EXT./INT. INTERCUT: RHONDA & STEVE BERNHARDT

Rhonda presses "Intercom" button on bathroom phone.

             RHONDA
    Who's there?

             STEVE BERNHARDT
    Flower delivery, ma'am.

             RHONDA
    Leave them at the door, please.

             STEVE BERNHARDT
    No can do, ma'am. I need a
    signature. Does a *Rhondy* Moreland
    live here?

             RHONDA
    Rhondy More-- who is this?

             STEVE BERNHARDT
    The card says "I'm fonda Rhonda."

             RHONDA
    Oh my God, is that--?

             STEVE BERNHARDT
    Yeah, it's me, sweetie-pie, Steve
    Bernhardt-used-to-be-Bucksbaum, and
    never, ever tell anybody that.

RHONDA
I can't believe it's you, Stevie!

STEVE BERNHARDT
Remembering Palm Springs days and
Coldwater Canyon nights. And Jeff
Corey's acting class. Man, I had
such a thing for you back then. I
think I still do.

RHONDA
La La Land was a long time ago,
Stevie. Fifteen years?

STEVE BERNHARDT
Way too long. Anyways, I'm doing
some freelance producing for HBO
Films, and Celebrity Hotline sent
me here to get an interview--

RHONDA
I've seen a lot of your stuff, it's
really good. Did my brother-in-law
David call you? For James?

STEVE BERNHARDT
No, this one's all about you, kid.
Lemme in so we can talk. And so I
can see you.

RHONDA
I'm not really presentable. Talk to
me now.

STEVE BERNHARDT
Well, for starters, the suits over
at HBO love your journey, and,
while I know you're not doing the
acting thing anymore, they want my
company to option the rights to
your story, and they want you to
test for the script lead. For you
to play you. You up for that?

Rhonda's demeanor shifts into professional
actress mode.

>   RHONDA
> Are you serious? I'm so flattered.

>   STEVE BERNHARDT
> Hundred per cent. But even more
> important, Rhondy? I wanna lay my
> eyes on that gorgeous face of yours
> again. "And what a figgah!"
> Remember?

>   RHONDA
> Stevie, you are still the charmer.
> But what if I told you my husband
> was standing next to me right now?

>   STEVE BERNHARDT
> I know he's not. I waited 'til he
> left.

>   RHONDA
> Well, he'll be back soon, so this
> ain't gonna fly. Right now. Just...
> leave the flowers on the porch,
> with your card, and I'll call you.
> I-- I definitely will.

>   STEVE BERNHARDT
> Rhondy, c'mon, lemme in, for old
> times' sake. "I'm fonda Rhonda. I'm
> fonda Rhonda." I really am.

Rhonda twirls around, smiles at herself in the
mirror.

>   RHONDA
> I really can't.

>   STEVE BERNHARDT
> Rhondy, even if you don't wanna do
> the TV interview, even if you don't
> wanna do the screen test, that's

cool. Really. Call me anyway. You, Rhonda Moreland, are an amazingly powerful woman, not to mention beautiful... so, okay, I'll just--

Steve Bernhardt puts his card in the flower bouquet. The front door opens. Rhonda stands there in her robe.

> RHONDA
> Alright, Mr. DeMille, I'm ready for my close-up.

She beckons him to her. He picks up flower arrangement, enters the house.

She kicks the front door shut, with a flair.

INT. SCHOOL CAFETERIA - SAME DAY - AFTERNOON

Ben and Chloe sit alone at one end of a crowded lunch table.

> CHLOE
> Are you kidding me?

> BEN
> No. We used a flash. My dad's freaking, but I think it was my--

> CHLOE
> Ben, there was so much going on in that tunnel. *Lots* of cameras, lots of photographers, right? And they say a white Fiat Uno is probably what caused the crash, not your dad's camera.

SCOTT, 15, Chloe's older brother, a chubby bully, appears.

> CHLOE (CONT'D)
> What do you want, Scotty?

                    SCOTT
          Hey sis, I wanna talk to tire boy
          over here. Hey, Goodyear. Your
          dad's an actor, right?

                    BEN
          It's Goodrich. What's it to you?

                    SCOTT
          So how much dinero is he making
          from those interviews? My father
          said that your dad is a real, um,
          opportunistic something or other.
          What'd he say, Chloe?

                    CHLOE
          He did not!

                    BEN
          Chloe, your brother's a major a-
          hole. Bell's about to ring, I'm
          goin'. You comin'?

Ben gets up from table, walks away. Chloe
follows him, turns around to Scott, mouths
"idiot."

EXT. SCHOOL PARKING LOT - SAME TIME

James sits in his parked green BMW, with dark
tinted windows. Driver's window is open. ROCK
MUSIC plays on car radio.

Jessica sits nearby in her parked white
Mercedes. She notices James sitting in his car.

She touches up her makeup, gets out of her car.
She walks to BMW's passenger window, RAPS on
it. Window rolls down.

                    JAMES
               (surprised)
          Jessica? Hi.

She opens passenger door, gets in. Locks the
door.

INT. JAMES'S BMW, PARKED - CONTINUOUS

She rolls window up.

                    JESSICA
          I've been seeing you all over TV
          this week, James Goodrich. You're
          like this handsome movie star, I
          never realized--

She moves closer to him, touches his arm.

                    JAMES
          Too bad not everybody thinks so.

Jessica touches his thigh. Her hand moves
slowly toward his crotch. James puts his hand
on top of hers.

                    JESSICA
          What do you mean? You're a
          celebrity. Everybody's talking
          about you. All the money you must
          be making. And did I tell you how
          handsome you look on TV? Wink!

                    JAMES
          Jesus, Jessica, we haven't accepted
          a dime. Would we be any better than
          the paparazzi if we did?

                    JESSICA
          Ya know, that's just what I told
          Norman. He thought you were raking
          it in. You are such a straight up
          guy, James Goodrich.

Her hand reaches his crotch.

> JESSICA (CONT'D)
> Yes, you are!

She giggles, unzips his fly, puts her hand down his pants.

> JESSICA (CONT'D)
> *So* good looking on TV. I bet you'll get lots of acting parts now.

> JAMES
> Don't. Ohh. Ya think so? Oh my--

> JESSICA
> Uh huh. So. Was it an accident or a conspiracy, what do you think? Norman was saying he heard that--

James removes Jessica's hand.

> JAMES
> Jessica, stop, it's the school parking lot, I can't do this. We're both married, the kids'll be here in a minute, and--

The school bell RINGS. Noisy STUDENTS exit school, CHATTERING.

Jessica sits up straight. James zips up his fly.

> JESSICA
> That was the appy, Mr. Movie Star. Call me. Cell number's on the back.

Jessica slips a business card in James's shirt pocket, kisses him lightly on his cheek. She opens her door, gets out of BMW. Ben and Chloe appear.

Ben enters BMW, shuts the door.

Chloe follows Jessica to white Mercedes. Scott joins them.

                    BEN
    Chloe's mother has a crush on you,
    huh?

                    JAMES
    Ya think?

INT. JAMES'S BMW - 1 MINUTE LATER

James is introspective as he drives down the
street.

                    BEN
    Still thinking about the camera?

James gives Ben a sideways glance.

                    JAMES
    Why do you ask?

                    BEN
    Maybe it was my fault.

                    JAMES
    Ben, you and I had nothing to do
    with... look, Henri Paul was trying
    to avoid this Fiat, right? That's
    what caused the crash, right? Isn't
    that what they're saying?

                    BEN
    That's what they're saying.

                    JAMES
    Okay, then.

They ride in silence.

                    BEN
    Did you get the film developed?

                    JAMES
    No. Just decided to trash it.

                    BEN
            (not buying it)
       Uh huh.

The Celebrity Hotline van passes by in opposite
direction.

James turns car radio on.

                    RADIO NEWSCASTER (V.O.)
       ...as investigation into the death
       of Princess Diana continues. And
       sources say that local eyewitness
       to the crash James Goodrich is a
       professional bit actor. They say
       there may be ulterior motives to
       his interviews, which may in fact
       compromise the validity of his
       testimony. Calls to his agent, his
       brother David Goodrich, have not
       been returned. In sports news--

James turns car radio off. They have arrived
home.

                    JAMES
       Your mother was right. Your uncle's
       an idiot. I'm gonna kill him. Go on
       inside, Ben. I have to run some
       errands.

EXT. 60 MINUTE PHOTO SHOP - MINUTES LATER

James parks BMW around the corner from shop.

INT. CUSTOMER AREA, 60 MINUTE PHOTO SHOP -
MOMENTS LATER

James walks into empty store.

> JAMES
> Anybody here? Hello? Picking up a
> film order for Bob Snyder. Hello?

> PHOTO SHOP EMPLOYEE (O.S.)
> One minute, Mr. Good-- Mr. Snyder.
> Just finishing 'em up.

INT. DEVELOPING ROOM, REAR OF SHOP - MOMENTS
LATER

PHOTO SHOP EMPLOYEE, late teens, has a
newspaper article on his desk about Princess
Diana, Henri Paul, the Goodrichs...

Next to it, a glossy photo of a very frightened
Henri Paul staring directly into the camera.

Photo Shop Employee gathers photo order, walks
through door.

INT. CUSTOMER AREA - CONTINUOUS

Photo Shop Employee enters.

> PHOTO SHOP EMPLOYEE
> Here ya go, sir. Twenty-six bucks
> even.

James hands him a $50 bill.

> JAMES
> Keep the change. Appreciate it.

> PHOTO SHOP EMPLOYEE
> Oh wow, thanks Mister... you *are*
> Mr. Goodrich, right?

> JAMES
> Yeah. Can you keep that quiet?

PHOTO SHOP EMPLOYEE
For sure.

James hands him a $100 bill and exits the
store, stat.

EXT. JAMES'S BMW - 1 MINUTE LATER

James leans against driver's door, thumbs
through packet of photos, removes three of
them. Looks at them intently.

JAMES
Knew it.

He puts the three photos in his jacket pocket,
gets into the BMW, drives away.

EXT. 60 MINUTE PHOTO SHOP - MINUTES LATER

Laurent, in full French police uniform, skids
his black Mercedes to a stop, exits his car,
runs inside.

INT. BANK SAFE DEPOSIT VAULT - SAME TIME

James puts negatives from film order into safe
deposit box, along with Paris police cap and
police badge.

INT. CUSTOMER AREA - MOMENTS LATER

Photo Shop Employee stands behind counter.
Laurent flashes French Police ID.

MONSIEUR LAURENT
I am here for the Goodrich film.
Official business. We spoke on the
phone yesterday, oui?

                    PHOTO SHOP EMPLOYEE
          Right. Actually, you spoke to my
          assistant Greg. Mr. Goodrich was,
          like, just here? He left with his
          pictures a few minutes ago. He used
          the name Snyder, but I knew--

                    MONSIEUR LAURENT
          Imbécile! I told this, this Greg,
          those photos are top secret--

                    PHOTO SHOP EMPLOYEE
          Oh hey, not a biggie, sir. Greg made
          a copy for you. It's in the back.

They start to walk into rear of store.

                    PHOTO SHOP EMPLOYEE (CONT'D)
          So how many photo stores did you
          have to call before you tracked us
          down? You are one badass detective.

INT. DEVELOPING ROOM, REAR OF SHOP - CONTINUOUS

They enter. Photo Shop Employee gives Laurent
the photo of Henri Paul staring directly into
the camera.

The white Fiat Uno is in foreground. The top of
a derby, Jacques, Laurent are blurry but
visible inside the car.

Paris police cap, worn backward, with police
badge, affixed, stands out clearly.

                    PHOTO SHOP EMPLOYEE
          Here ya go, officer.

Laurent looks at photo.

                    MONSIEUR LAURENT
          Good. Now give me the other one.

                    PHOTO SHOP EMPLOYEE
          There is no other one.

                    MONSIEUR LAURENT
          What?

                    PHOTO SHOP EMPLOYEE
          You told Greg you wanted the one
          with Henri Paul, right?

Laurent aims his gun at Photo Shop Employee's
head. Photo Shop Employee faints.

                    MONSIEUR LAURENT
          Aaagh, Americans!

He puts gun away, leaves store. Not a happy
Frenchman.

INT. JAMES'S LAWYER'S OFFICE - SAME TIME

James sits in chair opposite LAWYER. Three
photos are neatly laid out on the mahogany wood
desk between them.

INT. GOODRICH HOUSE, LIVING ROOM - LATER - DUSK

Chloe, clearly shaken, sits on piano bench next
to Ben, who plays CANDLE IN THE WIND. Poorly.
He hits a few sour notes.

Ben hears the kitchen door SQUEAK. He stops
playing.

                    BEN
          Dad?

                    JAMES (O.S.)
          Sounding pretty good there, Ben.
          Hey, Chloe.

Beat. No response.

JAMES (O.S.) (CONT'D)
Whose Mercedes is in the driveway?
Everything copacetic in here?

James enters the room. He sees Laurent, sitting
in a nearby chair, gun on lap. He sees Rhonda,
gagged, tied to a chair, hands tied behind her.

MONSIEUR LAURENT
It does not sound "pretty good
there," monsieur. In fact, it
stinks, you should give the boy
lessons. Where are the photos?

JAMES
My lawyer has them. How did you--?

The phone RINGS. James makes eye contact with
Ben, who reflexively presses the nearby phone's
"Speaker On" button.

BEN
(softly)
Hello?

MONSIEUR LAURENT
(in French, to Ben)
What are you doing? Hang that up!

JEFF SMITH'S VOICE (V.O.)
Hi, I'm Jeff Smith, a producer at
ABC News. Is Mr. Good--

The DOORBELL RINGS.

BEN
Hold on. Dad, what should--?

The DOORBELL RINGS again.

JAMES
Just wait, Ben.
(to Laurent)

I should answer the door. Lights
are on, cars are in the driveway.
People know we're home.

Ben whispers to Chloe, she nods. Laurent looks
at them.

> MONSIEUR LAURENT
> (whispers, agitated)
> Then answer it. Get rid of whoever
> it is, fast, or she dies, and so do
> these little brats.

James walks to front door.

> JEFF SMITH'S VOICE (V.O.)
> Is James Goodrich there. Hello?

Laurent, aware he is losing control, stands up,
gun in hand. He moves towards front door. Ben
sneaks away, out of sight.

> JAMES
> (loudly)
> Right here, Jeff. Gimme a minute.

Laurent's attention is riveted on the front
door. James opens it. Ben reappears behind an
oblivious Laurent. Ben nods to Chloe.

> CHLOE
> (to Laurent, loudly)
> Oh my God. Look at this. Over here!

Laurent turns his full attention to Chloe.

> AMERICAN
> POLICEMAN #2
> Mr. Goodyear, Officer
> McBain, Fourth
> Precinct. Is
> everything alright?
> Your neighbor called.
> She was walking her

> JEFF SMITH'S
> VOICE (V.O.)
> Sorry, I wasn't sure
> if you were talking
> to me. Okay. We saw
> you and your wife on
> Good Morning America
> and you guys came

dog past your house and heard a woman screaming. Is your wife okay? You look pretty shaken, sir, is everything--?

across so great, so heartfelt, especially your wife. I imagine you'll both be watching Diana's funeral on TV tomorrow?

Ben leaps onto Laurent from behind, tripping up his legs. Laurent falls down, face-first, still holding onto his gun. Ben quickly moves out of the way, and out of sight.

Laurent, on the floor, takes aim. He shoots at American Policeman #2. He misses.

American Policeman #2 shoots back, hits Laurent squarely between the eyes. Laurent is dead.

Chloe runs to Rhonda, takes gag out of her mouth. Ben unties Rhonda's arms and legs. She is visibly shaking.

American Policeman #2 steps into the house with James. They survey Laurent's dead body.

> JAMES
> Nice shot, three pointer. By the way, name's Goodrich. James Goodrich.

Rhonda SOBS. James goes to her, holds her tight.

> JEFF SMITH'S VOICE (V.O.)
> (sells it)
> Yes, I know that, sir. So, uh, let me get right to the point here, Mr. Goodrich. We'd like to come to your house with a TV crew tomorrow morning and set up a few cameras in your living room so that people all over the world can watch you and your family on TV as you and your family watch the funeral on TV,

that kind of thing. We'd like to
capture your reactions live, you
know, share your emotions with the
world. Think we can arrange
that...? Mr. Goodrich? Hello? Are
you there, sir? Hel--

Ben presses "End Call" button. Chloe walks
towards him.

> CHLOE
> You rock, man. You were so--

She gives him a fast peck on the lips, hugs
him. Ben grins, hugs her back.

> BEN
> Are you kidding me? "Oh my God.
> Look over here!" That was amazing,
> Chloe. You and me, we saved the
> day... like He-Man and She-Ra.

The phone RINGS many times. It goes unanswered.

INT. BRUNO'S ITALIAN RESTAURANT - WEEKS LATER -
NIGHT

TITLE OVER: 2 WEEKS LATER

BRUNO, 60's, owner and host, greets Rhonda with
a kiss on each cheek, an embrace for James.

> BRUNO
> (in a Jersey accent)
> Signore, signora, so *honored* to
> have ya here tonight. I got a nice
> private table in the back so you
> can be incognito-like.

Rhonda, James, Bruno walk past CUSTOMERS at
other tables.

Jessica is there with her husband NORMAN, late 50's, stocky build, and FOUR COUPLES. They are enjoying martinis.

                    NORMAN
              (drunkenly obnoxious)
         Hey looky, it's the local celebs.

Jessica, Norman, Four Couples applaud. Norman is boisterous. Rhonda and James, maintaining composure, smile and keep walking.

James shakes his head in feigned astonishment. He observes Rhonda, who waves to Customers at yet a different table.

                    JESSICA
         Hello Goodrichs. How you doin'?
         Still getting hounded?

                    RHONDA
         You mean like right now?

                    NORMAN
         Oh, Jimmy, can I have a autography,
         please?

Jessica shoves Norman playfully. Four Couples CHUCKLE.

                    JAMES
         Yeah. Here's my autography, Norman.

James gives him the finger. Everybody laughs. Except Norman.

                    NORMAN
              (under his breath)
         Fuckin' glory hound.

Rhonda and James follow Bruno to their private table.

                    BRUNO
     And lemme getcha coupla drinks on
     the house. What's your poison?

                    JAMES
     Oh, nice Bruno, thanks. Make it two
     Diet Cokes. On the rocks.

Bruno pulls out Rhonda's and James's chairs.
They sit. Bruno gives a quick glance towards
Norman's table.

                    BRUNO
     Comin' right up. And dinner's on
     the house, too. You guys are so
     great. Buono appetito!

Bruno signals to JAVIER, 30's, the waiter, who
brings some bruschetta to their table.

Rhonda digs in as Javier walks away.

                    JAMES
     It's amazing.

                    RHONDA
     This bruschetta is amazing. You're
     amazing. You loving your job?

                    JAMES
     Those assholes over there. They've
     always hated me, ya know? Ignored
     me like their shit don't stink. And
     now, all the sudden they wanna
     touch, like a "brush with
     greatness" kind of thing? My new
     best friends, so transparent and so
     fuckin' pathetic.

                    RHONDA
     I love you, honey. And Daddio is so
     happy you joined the company.

James sees Jessica looking at him. He waves.
She waves back.

> JAMES
> Look at that Jess, will ya? Stuck
> up bitch, right? Well, you won't
> even believe this, babe, but at my
> AA meeting last week, during the
> break, she was like, all over me.
> And Bruno, buying dinner for us
> tonight, it's so--

Rhonda turns in Jessica's direction.

> RHONDA
> Wait a minute, slow down. *"Jess?"*
> "All over you?"

James's cell phone RINGS. Just in time.

> JAMES
> Es mi hermano.

He flips the cell phone open. Javier arrives
with the Cokes.

> JAMES (CONT'D)
> Davy boy!
> (listens)
> Uh huh... good news... with a
> caveat... okay... yep, she's here.

He presses the phone's "Speaker" button.

> JAMES (CONT'D)
> Speaker's on. Talk.

> DAVID GOODRICH'S VOICE (V.O.)
> Caveat first, Jimbro. You're way
> too controversial for Coke, they
> yanked the campaign today. Hey,
> wasn't paying the bills anyway,
> right? Sorry, man. But... I got me

some great news for *Rhondy*. Hello
there, *Rhondy*.

          RHONDA
Hello there, *Davy*.

          DAVID GOODRICH'S VOICE (V.O.)
Rhon, I just got off the phone with
Bernhardt Productions. You met with
Steve a couple weeks ago?

James eyes her curiously. She eyes him back.

          RHONDA
Talk, David.

          DAVID GOODRICH'S VOICE (V.O.)
Well, it was kind of weird. He kept
referring to you as "Rhondy."
Anyways, his company has a firm
deal with HBO Films to produce a
movie about what happened to you
guys in Paris, but... and this is a
big but... HBO is sold, only if you
play you. And we're talkin' big
buckos here, kiddies. And Jimbro,
guess who's gonna play you? Ruce
Billis! Like, how crazy is that?

          JAMES
It's a thigh-slapper, David.

          DAVID GOODRICH'S VOICE (V.O.)
But wait, there's more! They're
talking producer credits for you on
the film, Jimbro. Plus, we have a
book deal with a huge advance from
Harper-Collins, and I'm a-smellin'
S-E-V-E-N figures here, kids! We
have a meeting in the city next
week.

James covers the cell phone's mouthpiece.

JAMES
You met with Steve Bernhardt?

RHONDA
No. Bucksbaum. Stevie Bucksbaum.

She looks at him, all wide-eyed and innocent.

JAMES
"Rhondy?"

RHONDA
(shrugs)
He's my Jessica. Rabbit.

She downs her Diet Coke. James sees a drunken Norman staggering towards him.

JAMES
(into phone)
Sounds good, Davy, we'll talk more tomorrow. But I gotta go, dessert's about to be served. Go celebrate, have some coke and a smile.

He snaps the flip phone shut.

JAMES (CONT'D)
(to his cell phone)
Order taker.

Javier appears.

JAVIER
(eager to please)
Yes, Meester?

JAMES
No no, not you, Javier.
(whispers, to Rhonda)
Seven figures? It's a start.

Rhonda smiles. Norman confronts James.

                    NORMAN
        Screw around with my wife, will ya?

                    JAMES
        Would I do that? First of all--

Norman picks him up by the collar, takes a
drunken swing, misses. James punches him
squarely in the jaw.

Norman staggers backwards and crashes on top of
an empty table, then ends up on the floor.
Bruno appears.

                    BRUNO
              (to Norman)
        You! Pay your check and get outta
        here. I knew you were trouble.

                    NORMAN
              (to James)
        Opportunistic son of a bitch!

James and Rhonda nod at each other. They stand
up, he puts a tip on the table, they start to
walk towards exit door.

Jessica, on her way to Norman, is about to walk
in front of them.

                    RHONDA
        And even more opportunity.

Rhonda puts her leg out, trips Jessica. She
goes flying, flailing, falls to the floor.
Right next to Norman.

                    RHONDA (CONT'D)
        Oh look Jim, Mrs. Transparent meets
        Mr. Pathetic. Bruno dear, we'll be
        back tomorrow night.

END OF ACT III.

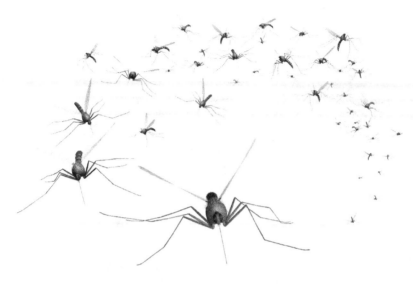

EPI-
LOGUE
August 1998

Paris & New York

INT. AIRPORT MANAGER'S OFFICE - DE GAULLE
AIRPORT - DAY

TITLE OVER: AUG. 1998, 1 YEAR LATER, PARIS

Rhonda, James, Airline Exec #1 enter. Airport
Manager, Airline Exec #2, Interpol Agent
approach.

                    INTERPOL AGENT
                (to Rhonda and James)
            Passports, s'il vous plait. You are
            both under arrest. For fraud.

Rhonda and James stare at each other in jaw-
dropping shock.

        RHONDA   JAMES
    Fraud? Are you out of   Fraud? Don't you know
    your mind?   who she is?

                    INTERPOL AGENT
            Your plane tickets are counterfeit.

                    RHONDA
            Impossible. I got them from the
            Oprah show. I'm Rhonda Goodrich.

She gets no response.

                    RHONDA (CONT'D)
            I'm here to do a TV interview for
            the one year anniversary of Diana's
            death. Show him my book, Jim.

                    JAMES
            They're all packed.

                    RHONDA
            Oh God.

                    INTERPOL AGENT
You will be taken into custody. The
return flight has been cancelled.

                    AIRPORT MANAGER
This is quite a serious charge.
Passports, if you please.

James takes two passports from his inner jacket
pocket, gives them to Interpol Agent. Interpol
Agent scans them.

His cell phone RINGS. He answers it.

                    INTERPOL AGENT
Yes, lieutenant. They are here.

He listens, then snaps the flip phone shut.

                    INTERPOL AGENT (CONT'D)
He's ready for you.

Interpol Agent handcuffs James's right hand to
Rhonda's left.

INT. MAIN TERMINAL, DE GAULLE AIRPORT - MINUTES
LATER

The Goodrichs and Interpol Agent walk through
terminal. James is in shock. Rhonda is in
tears.

INT. OUTSIDE "AUTHORIZED PERSONNEL ONLY" ROOM -
CONTINUOUS

Interpol Agent, key in hand, unlocks, then
opens, the door.

                    INTERPOL AGENT
               (in French)
Step inside. Now.

They just stand there. He pushes them into room, throws their passports in after them, quickly shuts door.

Interpol Agent locks door, stands guard outside room.

INT. "AUTHORIZED PERSONNEL ONLY" ROOM - CONTINUOUS

Gerard Barbette, unshaven, dishevelled, as we first met him on page 2, stands in room's center. He picks up passports.

Jacques and Monique, with poodle, sit in a corner.

Two empty hard-backed chairs in room's center, harsh lights shining down from above. Rhonda and James exchange glances.

>   MONIQUE
>   Hello again, monsieur, good to see
>   you. Welcome to our family meeting.

Jacques lunges to attack James. Barbette restrains him.

>   GERARD BARBETTE
>   (in French)
>   Easy, frére Jacques. Sit down, wait
>   for my say-so. Then we will both
>   have our revénche.

Jacques sits back down, smiles broadly at James, repeatedly smacking a fist from one hand into the palm of the other.

Barbette motions Rhonda and James to sit in the chairs.

>   GERARD BARBETTE (CONT'D)
>   So, tell me. How is little Benjy?

171

                    JAMES
Wait a minute. He's your...? You're
brothers?

                    GERARD BARBETTE
Step-brothers. What is it they say?
          (shrugs, laughs)
You can choose your friends, but...

Monique blows a kiss to Barbette, he blows one
back.

She kisses Jacques' cheek. Jacques wipes it
away, stands up.

                    GERARD BARBETTE (CONT'D)
I said sit down, *step*-brother.

Jacques remains standing. Barbette ignores him.

                    GERARD BARBETTE (CONT'D)
          (clears his throat)
Counterfeit tickets have nothing to
do with this meeting.

James stands up, drags handcuffed Rhonda
towards door. Barbette unholsters his gun.

          JAMES   RHONDA
   Come on Rhonda, let's   Ow! James, you're
   go. I knew it, this   hurting me! Stop
   is such a bunch of--   pulling me! Owww!
                            Jesus! Jim--

Barbette SHOOTS at ceiling. Rhonda and James
freeze in their tracks.

                    GERARD BARBETTE
Room is soundproofed. Sit down, you
are safer in here. My friend
outside? He has orders to kill.

Barbette circles Rhonda and James, slowly, like
a shark. His gun is pointed at them.

                    GERARD BARBETTE (CONT'D)
But, who knows? I may have to do it
for him. Or maybe, maybe I will
give the honor to frére Jacques.

Barbette laughs. Jacques and Monique laugh.

The poodle jumps off Monique's lap, runs to
James, nips at his heels. Rhonda and James back
away, take their seats.

Barbette puts gun down. He picks up poodle,
pets it.

                    GERARD BARBETTE (CONT'D)
You have been on my watch list
since you left Paris last year.

                    JAMES
Watch list? What does that even
mean? What do you--

                    GERARD BARBETTE
Revénche! Reprimanded by my
superiors, demoted to staff
lieutenant, laughed at by my peers,
ridiculed by my wife... all because
of you.
          (beat)
What I want, monsieur, is justice,
an eye for an eye. You murdered my
step-father, you ruined my career--

                    JAMES
He was killed by a New York cop.
You know that.

                    GERARD BARBETTE
Do not mince my words, you are a
very good liar. You also told me
you took no pictures in the tunnel
that night and I believed you.

Barbette takes a photo from his vest pocket, throws it towards James.

This is a copy of the photo that was picked up by James, and then by Laurent, at the 60 Minute Photo Shop last year. It's the photo of Henri Paul, staring directly into the camera from his black Mercedes. In the foreground is a white Fiat Uno, the top portion of a derby, and two blurred occupants, which could possibly be Jacques in front passenger seat, Laurent in rear seat. In better focus is the Paris police cap, with police badge affixed, worn backward on the head of rear seat passenger.

> GERARD BARBETTE (CONT'D)
> This photo, from *your* film order,
> was found in my step-father's
> Mercedes. In your driveway.
> Explain.

> JAMES
> My camera went off by accident--

> JACQUES
> (in French)
> Gerard, let me at him already!

Barbette ignores him. Barbette gives poodle to Monique.

> GERARD BARBETTE
> (laughs)
> By accident? Of course!
> (deadly serious)
> I will shoot you for this.

> JAMES
> ...but it was no accident that
> killed Diana and Dodi. They were
> *murdered* by the people in that
> Fiat. And I can prove it.

Jacques looks guiltily at Monique.

GERARD BARBETTE
Go on.

James reaches inside his jacket pocket.
Barbette picks up his gun, takes a shooter's
stance.

JAMES
Gerard. May I call you Gerard? The
only "weapon" I have here is the
proof I told you about. The proof
is in the proofs.

Barbette gulps, nods slightly. James removes an
envelope with two photos, puts them on nearby
table.

One of the photos is of the paparazzi in front
of the rear entrance to the Ritz, the afternoon
of the Goodrich's arrival in Paris a year ago.
It clearly shows Jacques... and Laurent, in
full police uniform, wearing the Paris police
cap, with police badge affixed to the cap, worn
backward. Photo auto-dated: **AUG 30 1997 05:41
P.M.**

The other photo is a computer enhanced copy of
Barbette's photo, but in ultra-sharp focus,
detailing faces very meticulously: Jacques in
front passenger seat, Laurent in rear seat.
Photo auto-dated: **AUG 31 1997 12:22 A.M.**

Barbette studies James's two photos.

JAMES (CONT'D)
Computer enhanced. Direct your
attention to the Paris police cap
and badge, Gerard. The gift you
gave Benjy. Recognize anybody?

Monique watches this interplay intently.

Barbette holsters his gun. He walks to Jacques,
shoves the three photos in his face.

> GERARD BARBETTE
> (in French, to Jacques)
> What the fuck is this?
> (to James)
> And you hope to prove what with
> these pictures, monsieur?

> JAMES
> Call me James, please. Gerard... my
> friend... your secret is out but
> it's safe with me. It's safe with
> my lawyer in New Yo--

> GERARD BARBETTE
> But I have no secret. I never knew
> *any* of this. L'irrationnel!

> JAMES
> The truth has no agenda, Gerard.
> Look. Here is the money shot.

James reaches into his inside jacket pocket,
pulls out one more photo. The picture that
James took in Barbette's office a year ago,
with Marie Tiessart, Interpreter, Barbette and
Ben posing. Ben wears the Paris police cap,
backward, and is holding out the Paris police
badge towards the camera. Photo auto-dated: **SEP
01 1997 09:06 P.M.**

Barbette is in shock.

He moves closer to Monique and Jacques, grabs
Jacques by the shoulders.

> GERARD BARBETTE
> (in French, to Jacques)
> Did your father try to implicate me
> because I was just his *step*-son?
> Wait, *your* step-*brother*! Was that
> it? Maybe it was *your* idea all
> along, yes?

Jacques escapes Barbette's hold, runs to the door.

> JACQUES
> This had nothing to do with you, I swear it! They offered us a million pounds, Gerard, a million pounds to kill the Sphinx. So we killed him. And the bastards refused to pay up. Let me out of here!

> MONIQUE
> Jacques and his imbécile father were supposed to use the *camera-gun* to kill the Sphinx. They failed.

Monique walks to Jacques, spits in his face.

> MONIQUE (CONT'D)
> Crétin!

The poodle BARKS and SNARLS at Jacques.

> GERARD BARBETTE
> Camera-gun? What are you--

Jacques is on the verge of tears. Monique walks back to her seat, removes a damp blue rag from her purse.

> JACQUES
> But we caused the crash, mother, so we *did* kill him, we deserved to get paid but they--

> GERARD BARBETTE
> (to Monique)
> Who is this "they?"

She shifts in her seat.

> MONIQUE
> I do not know, Gerard.

> GERARD BARBETTE
>
> Enough of this psycho babble.

Barbette paces back and forth. He removes his gun from its holster, takes direct aim at Monique.

> MONIQUE
>
> Gerard. No!

Monique shields her face with the poodle.

> GERARD BARBETTE
>
> What kind of brother are you, Jacques, who brings such shame to his family? Get away from the door right now or I will kill her.

Jacques BANGS repeatedly on the door.

> GERARD BARBETTE (CONT'D)
>
> You are a good for nothing sack of shit. You killed a beloved Princess and her boyfriend, then tried to implicate me. And you'd even have me kill our own mother just to save your worthless ass. You're as bad as Laurent. The apple doesn't fall far. God forgive me.

Barbette shoots Jacques in the back. He falls over, dead.

Monique sobs. Rhonda gasps. James holds her tightly.

> GERARD BARBETTE (CONT'D)
> (in English, to Monique)
>
> I am not afraid to use this again. When we leave here you are to show no emotion. Do you understand me?

She nods her head, continues to cry.

                    GERARD BARBETTE (CONT'D)
          Then stop that weeping. Arrête!

She stops. Barbette drags Jacques' dead body
away from door.

                    GERARD BARBETTE (CONT'D)
          So now, what should we do with
          you... James?

                    JAMES
          Drop these trumped up charges and
          let us go. And we didn't see a
          thing. As I said, your secrets are
          safe.

                    GERARD BARBETTE
          Then we are *both* innocent?

                    JAMES
          You and me? Gerard, we were never
          guilty.

Barbette stares at photos.

                    JAMES (CONT'D)
          Go ahead, you can rip 'em up or
          keep 'em. My lawyer has got access
          to the negatives. If need be.

Barbette nods his head. He rips up the photos,
puts the pieces in his pocket, unlocks their
handcuffs, opens the door.

The four of them, and the poodle, exit room.

INT. NEAR "AUTHORIZED PERSONNEL ONLY" ROOM -
CONTINUOUS

Interpol Agent flips his cell phone closed.

Barbette hands passports back to James.

GERARD BARBETTE
(to Rhonda and James)
...and I apologize for this small
inconvenience. I will look into
your story with the TV show and
contact you at the Ritz. If need
be.

Barbette bows to them. James nods. Rhonda sobs
quietly, holds James tightly around his waist.

Barbette turns away from Goodrichs, reaches
into his pocket, covertly pulls out a large wad
of bills.

He palms the money to Interpol Agent, who
pockets it.

GERARD BARBETTE (CONT'D)
(in French, whispers)
The Americans are free to go. Take
care of the mess inside. I never
liked him anyway. A loose cannon.

Interpol Agent nods, enters "Authorized
Personnel Only" room.

RHONDA
Jim, call the Oprah producer.
Cancel it. We should go home today.

GERARD BARBETTE
Yes, I think that might be best.

Interpol Agent shuts the door. The lock CLICKS.
James nods.

GERARD BARBETTE (CONT'D)
There is a plane that leaves for
New York in a few hours. I can
arrange safe passage. Meet me at
the Airport Manager's office... in
thirty minutes.

Barbette takes Monique by the hand, walks away, then stops in his tracks. He turns around, salutes James.

                    GERARD BARBETTE (CONT'D)
          You are a good man, my friend James
          Goodrich. And a very good father.

James nods.

Barbette and Monique turn away, begin walking again.

                    GERARD BARBETTE (CONT'D)
                    (in French, whispers)
          They know way too much, mother.

                    MONIQUE
          Yes they do. And a very enjoyable
          show, my sweet Gerard. You would
          make a fine actor.

Monique gives him a key.

                    MONIQUE (CONT'D)
          Here. It opens locker 8023. Your
          half is inside, my five hundred is
          secure at home.

The poodle BARKS.

Barbette's cell phone RINGS. He flips it open, listens.

                    GRAVELLY VOICE (V.O.)
          I spoke to your Interpol friend. I
          want the Americans taken out
          tomorrow, in the States. Be
          discrete. An auto accident seems to
          do the trick, but I will leave it
          to you. Another million awaits, on
          successful completion.

> GERARD BARBETTE
> Consider it done, your Lordship.

Barbette disconnects the call. He turns to
Monique.

> GERARD BARBETTE (CONT'D)
> I must call my man in New York.

INT. JUMBO JET, FIRST CLASS - LATER - DAY

Rhonda stares out the window. James sits next
to her, reading her book *"Getting Diana'd" by
Rhonda Goodrich*. Rhonda's photo is on the back
cover.

James looks at Rhonda for a moment. Is she
melancholic? He puts the book face down.

> JAMES
> You okay?

She nods, looks lovingly at him. He smiles back
gently.

> JAMES (CONT'D)
> Penny for your thoughts.

> RHONDA
> Seems a little pricey.

She turns in her seat, faces him directly.

> RHONDA (CONT'D)
> I am so proud to be your wife. You
> saved our lives. You played the
> part like the best actor in the
> world.

> JAMES
> No act, babe. I'd take a bullet for
> you. Really.

                    RHONDA
        You never said that to me before.

                    JAMES
        I just did.

They kiss passionately.

INT./EXT. JUMBO JET, BLUE SKY AND PUFFY CLOUDS
- LATER (RHONDA'S REVERIE)

Rhonda stares out window. Her eyes slowly
close. She sees:

Princess Diana and Prince Charles wave from
their carriage... Diana and Charles show the
world their first born son... Diana holds an
AIDS baby... Diana walks through land mines...
Diana and Dodi Al Fayed walk through revolving
doors...

Her two young sons walk together during her
funeral procession.

INT. JUMBO JET - LATER

Rhonda awakens, turns to James. He's fast
asleep. She takes the open book off his lap.

She turns to the dedication page, looks at it.

                    RHONDA (V.O.)
        "...So nice to have known you,
        although we've not met."

She looks at the diamond bangle bracelet James
bought for her in England. She touches it,
smiles contentedly, reclines in her seat. She
closes her eyes.

She puts her hand on top of James's.

EXT. MAIN TERMINAL, JFK AIRPORT - HOURS LATER - DAY

TITLE OVER: 8 HOURS LATER, JFK AIRPORT, NEW YORK

Rogue Cop, unlit cigar butt dangling from corner of his mouth, eyes Rhonda and James as they exit terminal.

BAGGAGE HANDLER pulls large cart loaded with Goodrich's designer luggage.

ROGUE LIMO DRIVER, swarthy, menacing-looking, holds sign reading "Mr. and Mrs. Goodrich." He stands near parked black Mercedes limo, smiles in Rogue Cop's direction. He feels for his hidden gun in his coat's inside pocket.

Parked behind the black Mercedes limo is a queue of empty yellow-checkered taxicabs.

Rhonda stops in her tracks, looks at limo, looks at taxi. She walks to taxi, stands near pleasant-looking ROGUE TAXI DRIVER. Rhonda motions for James to join her.

> JAMES
> (to Rogue Limo Driver)
> I wear the pants in the family but
> she controls the zipper. Thanks,
> man.

James tips him. He and Baggage Handler proceed to taxi. James playfully gooses Rhonda. They laugh, a quick smooch. James gives Baggage Handler a tip. He smiles, exits.

Rogue Limo Driver approaches Rogue Cop. Both anxiously watch Rhonda, James, Rogue Taxi Driver from afar.

Rogue Taxi Driver loads luggage into trunk. He smiles in Rogue Cop's direction. Rogue Cop nods back. All good.

EXT. YELLOW TAXI - CONTINUOUS

Rogue Taxi Driver, all smiles, opens rear door. He feels for his hidden gun in his jacket's inside pocket. It's not there! His expression turns alarmed. Oh wait, it's in the *other* inside pocket. Phew!

He motions for the Goodrichs to enter taxi.

                    ROGUE TAXI DRIVER
          Where to, lovebirds?

Rhonda gets into rear seat. James is about to join her but is distracted by persistent horn HONKING.

EXT. AIRPORT ROAD NEAR TERMINAL - CONTINUOUS

David Goodrich drives a fiery red 4 Door Hummer H1, Suzy Q in front passenger seat. Ben and Chloe, sans hot-pink braces, sit in rear. All Hummer windows are open.

Hummer slowly passes the parked taxi. Ben snaps several photos with his camera, equipped with a "rapid-fire" flash.

                    BEN
          Mom! Dad! Say cheese!

                    SUZY Q
          Welcome home!

INTERCUT: One photo shows Rhonda, James, Rogue Taxi Driver in foreground, Rogue Cop and Rogue Limo Driver in background.

Rhonda exits parked taxi, joins James curb
side. They are thrilled to see everybody. Rogue
Taxi Driver, not thrilled.

                    SUZY Q
             (from moving Hummer)
        Ben insisted we surprise you.

                    JAMES
             (to Rogue Taxi Driver)
        Know what I did before I got
        married? Anything I wanted to.
        Thanks, man.

James hands Rogue Taxi Driver a tip.

Rogue Taxi Driver averts his eyes from camera
flashes. He's in a state of disbelief as he
unloads luggage.

Hummer slows to complete stop, parks in "No
Parking Zone." Ben opens door, runs to his
parents. Big family hug.

                    RHONDA
        I missed you so much.

David wears a T-shirt adorned with words "Yada
Yada Yada" on front. He, Suzy Q, Chloe exit
Hummer, greet Rhonda and James.

Rogue Taxi Driver looks towards Rogue Cop and
Rogue Limo Driver. Not a happy bunch.

A police SIREN WHOOPS three times. AMERICAN
POLICEMAN #3's squad car, lights flashing,
approaches.

Rogue Taxi Driver quickly gets in his taxi,
drives away. Rogue Limo Driver makes a beeline
for his limo, departs the terminal, post haste.
Rogue Cop disappears inside terminal.

James tenderly gazes into Rhonda's eyes, pulls her into a close embrace.

Chloe holds Ben's hand. Ben's grin widens. He discreetly wipes at his watery eyes as he watches his parents smooch.

> DAVID GOODRICH
> (to James)
> Knock knock, anybody home?

James ignores him.

> DAVID GOODRICH (CONT'D)
> Jimbro, I'm like "this close" to a re-book on Larry King next week.

> JAMES
> (kissing Rhonda)
> Bump 'em.

Suzy Q playfully hits David's arm. Rhonda laughs in relief.

> DAVID GOODRICH
> Ow! Yeah. Gotcha.

He reaches for Suzy Q, holds her close. American Policeman #3 appears, holds ticket book.

> AMERICAN POLICEMAN #3
> This is a "No Parking Zone," sir.

> DAVID GOODRICH
> And we were just leaving.

James and David hastily place luggage into trunk. Ben and Chloe get into Hummer's rear, Suzy Q gets in front.

American Policeman #3 walks back to his squad car.

David shuts trunk, hops into driver's seat, starts engine. Rhonda and James get into rear seat, next to Ben and Chloe.

INT. POLICE SQUAD CAR - CONTINUOUS.

Squad car remains parked, lights still flashing. American Policeman #3 takes a few digital photos of Hummer, including an extreme close-up of Hummer's license plate.

INT. HUMMER - MOMENTS LATER

                    BEN
          Dad, look at the camera Uncle Dave
          got me. One of those new digitals!

The police SIREN WHOOPS three more times. David is startled. He puts the Hummer in drive, pulls away.

                    DAVID GOODRICH
          Scared the freakin' crap outta me.

A lot of laughter as the Hummer drives off.

EXT. AIRPORT ROAD - MOMENTS LATER

American Policeman #3's squad car, lights still flashing, follows Hummer.

Hummer makes lefts and rights, squad car follows closely behind. This continues for a short while.

Hummer enters the main highway. Picks up speed.

Squad car turns off lights, drives away in opposite direction.

FADE TO BLACK.

TUNNEL
VISION

My personal journal concerning
the world-shaking event of 8/31/97

by Jack Firestone

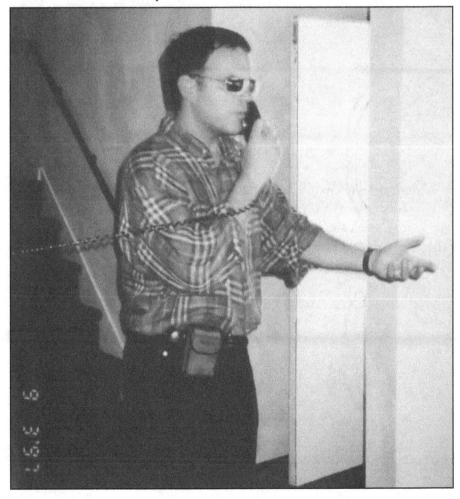

This is the private and personal journal of Jack Firestone...
just now being made public for the first time ever
in this 20 year memorial edition of

CHASING DIANA
Perception vs. Reality

Tunnel Vision © 2005 by Jack Firestone
© 2017 by the Firestone Living Trust

International Incident in a French Tunnel

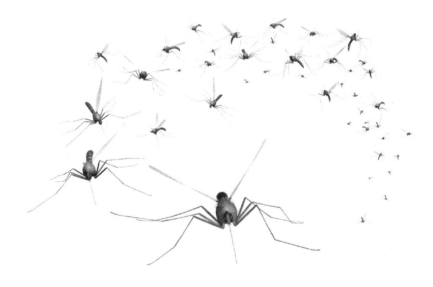

re·al·i·ty
rēˈalədē/

noun

- the state of things as they actually exist

Contents

*For Robin and Rhonda
and Brandon and Ben*

"The truth has no agenda"

TUNNEL
VISION
AMERICANS IN PARIS:
INTERNATIONAL INCIDENT IN A FRENCH TUNNEL

a journal by JACK FIRESTONE

ENCOUNTER...

The odds are 6 billion to one. The events we experience are far too incredible to have actually taken place. Please pinch me and wake me up from this awful dream.

And yet, here we are, wide-eyed tourists on what has, up to this point, been a fun-filled family vacation. Now we are three unwitting participants – captives, actually – as we sit helplessly in the back seat of a taxicab which speeds down a French avenue in the small hours of the morning, just minutes after midnight on Sunday, August 31st, 1997. And I realize, as our taxi driver suddenly slams on the brakes, that this is no bad dream at all. This is a horrible nightmare.

We are now in the middle of a bumper-to-bumper traffic jam, as other cars alongside us also crowd into a tunnel up ahead, and without realizing it, we are moments away from becoming witnesses to one of the world's most traumatic and shocking events in recent history, as it unfolds before our eyes: a tragedy of epic proportion.

Do you remember where you were when you heard the news that Princess Diana was killed? Most everybody has an answer... but nobody has an answer quite like ours.

Here's how it all came about:

GEOGRAPHY LESSON...

It starts off innocently enough. It's the middle of June, 1997, and my beautiful wife Robin, ever the sweet-talker, totally sweeps me up with her excitement as she starts to plan our family's first-ever trip to Europe. Always the big thinker, Robin has her mind made up from the get-go – despite my grudgingly ineffective protests – that our twelve-year-old son Brandon is going to join us as we three do the "Tour Of England" vacation thing in grand style. Robin tells me that she's already done her research and the cost of the tickets is very reasonable (she knows I like to hear that kind of stuff), and that leaving in late August is ideal, after Brandon gets home from summer camp and just before school begins. Robin is pitching a departure date that even coincides with my birthday, no less. "You deserve this, Jack," she says. "We'll have a great time, leave it to me. I'll take care of all the details." How could I resist such sweet-talking like that? Truth be told, I can't.

Not one to get too fired up about leaving the comfort of my hammock, however – no less my "home sweet home" – to my utter amazement and delight I find myself completely under Robin's spell and I share her enthusiasm! I think the idea actually has a lot of appeal; as a matter of fact, it sounds like it'll be another one of those awesome "Firestone Family Vacations" that we and our son have made a part of our family's culture for many years now. (National Lampoon, watch out: here come the Firestones!)

As the days slip by, Robin's gusto for this trip grows by leaps and bounds; it's contagious, in truth... and one evening, as we sip our martinis, I add my three cents. I insist that "Hey, if we're already gonna be in *one* country in Europe, then, while we're there, let's go to another country, too. A *nearby* country. Makes sense, right?" So, based purely on a mix of geography and vodka alone, it only stands to reason that we add neighboring Paris, France to the vacation itinerary mix. And so we do. (Okay, I have to listen to Robin protest about going to Paris for "*only three days!*" but this is one argument I win!)

Now the trip has all the makings of real adventure... and what an adventure it turns out to be...

Hey: you know that old saying, the one about being careful what you wish for, 'cause you just might get it? Well, we got it.

WHAT'S ON TV TONIGHT?...

Before we depart from New York, Robin and I debate whether or not I should bother taking the camcorder on the trip; those 1997 camcorders are heavy, bulky and cumbersome pieces of electronic equipment, so the thought of lugging it around in *two* foreign countries sounds more like a hassle than like fun. So I opt, instead, for my good ol' reliable 35mm camera, which I can keep tucked inside a camera case, neatly attached to my belt loop.

You know, it's curious how life works; more often than not it's totally unpredictable, and it often surprises us and takes us to places which are the very antithesis of our innocent and naïve expectations. Little did we know – how *could* we know – that, when we arrive home from Paris ten days later on September 2nd, airing on TV will be a lot of videos (taken with *other* peoples' video cameras, no less) of both London and Paris, broadcast from all over the world. We are even *in* some of these news videos as the featured story. Yes, it's strange how life works... and that irony has never left me.

YOUR LEFT, YOUR LEFT, YOUR LEFT, RIGHT, LEFT...

And so it is that on Saturday, August 23rd (happy birthday to me), the three of us depart our suburban home for that vacation of a lifetime. Our plan is to fly across the pond and begin our journey with a week's stay in a small hotel in London called the White House. No kidding.

And all the while, of course, Robin has every single day's touring schedule planned out to an English "tea"... clotted cream included (this doesn't sound too good to me, but it is!)

We will begin our travels with a tour of the countryside – at breakneck speed, I might add – because we are following "Robin's Rule" (translation: "Cram in as much tourism as you can, 'cause we're only gonna be here for a week..." kind-of-thing, and the "We gotta keep moving, we have places to go, things to see, hurry up..." kind-of-thing.)

As I intimated earlier (see "comfort of my hammock" passage), I'm the kind of guy who likes to chill and just take it easy; I don't have nearly as much excitement and stamina as Robin does about site seeing: a couple of strolls around the hotel lobby to check out the gift shops, perhaps... and room service!... are more my style. But after a few days in London, what with Robin's insistence that we awaken everyday at 6:00 AM to get ready for the new day's touring schedule, her promise to me is that, when we arrive in Paris at week's end, we will definitely follow "Jack's Rule" (translation: We can cap off the trip with a few days of relaxation... "And I mean it, honey," says my lovely, so very convincingly. "*You deserve it,*" she says again.)

In the meantime, even though I know I'm gonna be enjoying this trip, (especially through the eyes of both Robin and Brandon), traipsing through England as we'll be doing... I can't help but compare it to one of those special sitcom episodes they used to show on TV, like when the show's entire cast travels abroad (think "*Married With Children* Goes to London.")

But by the time we arrive back on U.S. soil some ten days later, it is anything but comedic... it is heavy drama all the way; actually, we find ourselves cast as the central characters in an international murder mystery espionage action adventure thriller, replete with conspiracy, to boot.

THE ONLY WAY TO FLY...

Yet again I say, it's curious how life works: Robin and I often benefit from the "Law of Expectation" – I, in fact, ten years earlier, had won $25,000 on a $1 bet, having selected the correct numbers in a brand new New York State Lottery game, and I attributed those winnings to the fact that I *expected* to win big; that same week, in fact, as we had dined in a local seafood restaurant, I found a pearl in one of the oysters I was eating – and now I'm on a roll: yet again that same week, I had won a cool $1,000 in a horse raceway trifecta on a whim: I in fact demanded that Robin stop the car immediately so I could literally run into an Off Track Betting parlor we had just passed in order for me to place a fast $3 bet on some horses I selected at random – and, to this day, I always have parking spots waiting for me, too... simply because I *expect* them to be there, waiting for me. Robin and Brandon, I might add, subscribe to the same philosophy.

Being in the right place at the right time for Robin and me is much more frequent than rare... so, it's no surprise to us that, even though we only paid for roundtrip coach airfare from New York's JFK to London's Heathrow, we end up getting roundtrip upgrades to First Class, at no additional charge. (Leave it to Robin!)

The upgrades are due to two different blonde-haired women: the JFK to Heathrow First Class upgrade happens when a serendipitous encounter occurs with the mom of one of our son's friends; she just happens to work at American Airlines on the day and time we are there... and she just happens to have the power to bump us up, *gratis*. (Oh, how I long for the good old days of '97, when such things were still possible!)

Sadly, though, the return trip First Class upgrade, from Paris' de Gaulle to JFK, is courtesy of having bumped into the other blonde: the late, great Princess Di.

YANKEE DOODLES GO TO LONDON...

Anyway, I digress. Suffice it to say that the entire England portion of our trip is fantastic; we have the time of our lives:

We first arrive in London's Heathrow – bright and early, like 7:00 AM local time on the 24th of August – thoroughly exhausted, excited and exhilarated, all rolled into one.

Next stop, that charming boutique hotel called the White House... I remember two specific things about that place: [1] they serve a daily English breakfast that is, to put it kindly... yechhh! (unless you're a huge fan of blood sausage and kidney pie); and [2] our hotel room is much smaller than we expect (translation: it's a cubicle, Murphy bed and all)... *but* we convince ourselves that we will only be using the room for sleeping, so it's all good. And this happens to be true, because Robin has the three of us on the march, seemingly 24/7, all over England, to explore the sites.

I have to hand it to Robin: in the span of seven days we see and experience so much. (No rest for the weary, here.) We travel a lot via the tubes (subways), and for the next week we learn to "mind the gap" as well as any jolly ol' Englishman.

FOR TOURISTS ONLY...

Like the natives, we use the tubes to maneuver around London, and like the tourists, we take guided bus tours of the major attractions and the surrounding countryside. At Buckingham Palace, for instance, Robin just *has* to have me purchase a bracelet for her, designed especially for Princess Diana by the very "Crown Jeweler" himself! We travel to the likes of Piccadilly Circus and Oxford Circus (sorry kids, the clowns have all gone home)... we go to Covent Gardens, we enjoy Trafalgar Square, we shop at Harrods Department Store... Hamleys, the Tower of London, Banqueting House, Leeds' Castle, Stonehenge... we see it all! Did I mention Greenwich? Oh... we take a boat ride on the River Thames, we watch the Inspection of the Guards, we take in Big Ben, and ogle the actual Crown Jewels themselves. We tour Bath, Dover, Salisbury, and Canterbury, too. We enjoy an outdoor production of "Kiss Me, Kate!" in Regents Park, and we are audience to a London production of "Grease!" as well ('50's greasers with English accents? I just hadda see this.)

We never learned to like the blood sausage, though... but the authentic fish and chips, wrapped in newspaper, was jolly good indeed!

CHUCK & DI...

But seriously, can you imagine this schedule? And I'm not nearly finished... we ride on the double-decker busses. We drive by Kensington Palace and Windsor Palace and Westminster Abbey. We engage in conversations with the locals, on the streets and in the pubs, often getting their unbiased opinions about Charles and Diana. (Most everyone we talk to hates him, loves her... this is so amusing to us because all the townsfolk are so vocal about it!) And it is worthy of note that the biggest impression I am left with is this: the citizenry *thank* their lucky stars and feel so fortunate that Charles took *Diana* (and not some princesszilla) for his bride. Because you cannot, with much due respect to *my* princess Robin, get more likeable and more lovely than Lady Diana Spencer.

That's really what we experience overridingly... Princess Diana fever. She is simply the talk of the town... she is in the hearts and on the minds of every male and female red-blooded English citizen. The people of the United Kingdom are so in love with their Diana.

ENTER DODI AL FAYED...

On Thursday, August 28th, the three of us go to Harrods to eat some sushi, do "high tea," and (surprise!) do some shopping, too. As an avid "Beanie Baby" collector, Robin wants to see the assortment of "Beanie Babies" which have the U.K. tag on them; in particular, the special "Britannia The Bear" (a U.K. exclusive)... so we head to the store's toy department. Robin approaches one of the salesgirls, a young and lovely English bird – but nobody compares to my chick, Robin – named Dorothy. While Brandon roams the toy department's treasures, we three adults talk about Dodi Al Fayed (his father, Mohamed Al Fayed, owns Harrods) and his relationship with Princess Diana – again, that was "the" thing to talk about – and Dorothy says to us, "Oh, wouldn't it be just loverly [sic] if Dodi would go out with me! Then the newspapers would blare a headline: *'Dodi Drops Diana For Dorothy!'* Imagine that!" (*"Imagine that, indeed,"* I think sarcastically.) We all share a polite laugh, and Dorothy then excuses herself and minutes later presents Robin with the highly coveted "Britannia," which Robin still owns to this day. Good show, Dorothy... jolly good!

As we exit the store, Robin strikes up a conversation with the very bedecked "most tenured" elderly doorman (what a caricature!) in all of Harrods's history (he must be 103 if he's a day!) He's a real nice English gent, who shares with us his love of all things Diana. (As it was too good of a photo op to miss, I took a terrific picture of him posing with Robin and Brandon.)

Because of that tenure, it opens up a whole series of questions which Robin has about Princess Diana and her intended Dodi. Our regally uniformed doorman has met Diana many times, he tells us, and he too shares with us his stories about his admiration for Diana and his distaste for Charles. The British people's condemnation of

Charles as compared to their affection for Diana seems to be jolly good sport, and, as I stated earlier, is a politely acceptable societal topic (and, to my ears, anyway, a politely quaint one, at that.)

After several minutes of this banter with the doorman, we say our "cheerios" to him as we rush off – and arrive just in time – to watch the Changing of the Guard... followed up by a tour of Buckingham Palace. No doubt about it... I have to admit it... we *are* having fun!

WISH YOU WERE HERE...

It is later that night, in our room at the White House – I love how that sounds – as we get ready for bed, that I write several postcards to friends and family back home, including this one, which I send to a couple of secretaries in my office:

Thu 28/8/97

Dear Linda & Anna,

We're having a royally GREAT time here in the U.K.! Queen E. (and Di) send their love. Robin tried on the crown jewels. Have been to castles, palaces, & cathedrals galore! Went shopping at Harrods. Saw all the London sites! A lot more planned for Fri., then off to France on Sat. Wish you were here!

Love,

Robin, Jack, Brandon

I mean, we are totally immersed in the mother country culture! We love it! At this point, the three of us feel like honorary Brits ourselves... which only makes what happens, some forty-eight hours later, that much more sorrowful. What a difference a couple of days make, indeed.

ARE WE THERE YET?...

And so it is that, late in the morning on Saturday, August 30th, we depart London via the EuroStar Chunnel train for Paris, where we are to enjoy the last leg of our vacation: three nights in a luxurious one-bedroom suite at the Hotel Castille on the Rue Cambon. I am so ready for "Jack's Rule" to kick in... re-lax-a-tion, here I come, baby!... *Yes*!

The train ride is beautiful – I have to laugh at Brandon's boldness as he dons a Señor Frogs sweatshirt – not to be missed. It is a testament to man's ingenuity, by the way, to have created a marvel such as this; an underwater tunnel for travel between two countries! And after a scant couple hours or so, our train arrives in Paris about 2:00 PM local time (which, based on the time zone difference, is 1:00 PM London time), and after we retrieve our "way too many pieces" of luggage, we enter a tiny elevator to go to the street level to catch a taxi ride to our hotel.

At the street level, in order for me to exit the crowded elevator with our bags, I have to back out of it while pulling my suitcases toward me. Robin and Brandon have already told me that they'll meet me outside, in front, at the taxi stand, so now they're nowhere in sight.

As I exit the elevator, I must have accidentally bumped into an "unseen passenger," because moments later I feel a sharp jab in the middle of my back. I turn around and see a very elderly French lady – my "unseen passenger," no doubt – now revealed in all her *magnifique* glory. She curses loudly at me – in French, of course – and with audacity as such I've never before encountered, she continues to poke away at the small of my back with the tip of her umbrella... like she was sampling the density of a soufflé or something. (This, by the way, is what has become known to me as Nasty French Incident # 1.) Welcome to France, *mon ami*!

AMERICANS IN PARIS...

I walk over to the Foreign Money Exchange Booth to get French francs for my English pounds and American dollars. I have this tiny currency converter contraption on my person, which is supposed to make it easy to calculate English pounds to French francs... but I must admit I accidentally press some of the wrong buttons and mess it up, so it takes me a bit longer than it should have to figure out if I got the correct exchange rate. Turns out I did.

I then join Robin and Brandon, thinking that they'll be standing on line for a cab to take us to our hotel. But Robin had been approached by a well-dressed French limo driver, who offers us a ride to our hotel in his plush Mercedes sedan. Robin wants to take him up on his offer – she doesn't ask him what the offer is, dollar wise – and although I am reluctant, I agree to go along for the ride (this, and all the other bad puns throughout, are intentional, by the way.)

As Monsieur Driver loads our luggage into the trunk, though, I sense that something isn't kosher; what's bugging me is that he *never* mentions the cost of the fare, so I ask him what the price tag will be. He says, in that haughty French way, "Eet is *only* 350 francs, monsieur!"

I ask him how long of a ride it will be; he replies that "...eet ees only a fifteen minute ride, monsieur!" and he adds, with a trace of condescension, "zee 350 francs ees a much lezzer fare zan zee meter taxicabs charge!" Some quick math on my part has me figure the cost at about $125 U.S. – thanks to my now adept use of the trusty currency converter – which, especially in 1997, seems outrageous for a fifteen minute ride. I tell him so, and he "over-shrugs..." – not just a shrug, mind you, but an *over-shrug* – a shrug with *attitude*. There is something about this shrug that tells me we will be better served if I ask him to immediately unload the trunk... and I do. I tell him we prefer, instead, to wait on line for a meter cab, after all... to Robin's dismay, I might add. He snidely gives me a patronizing sneer, and, using a phony American accent, now says "Okay, *Jack*... whatever you want... *Jack!*" His use of my first name, which, of course, he has learned from Robin, is rather creepy. Perhaps I should have introduced him to Umbrella Lady. (This, by the way, is Nasty French Incident # 2 – keep score, there's lots more to come.) *Viva la France!*

As it turns out, we wait on line for only five minutes, and the meter cab ride is an absolute pleasure. Total cost: seventy-one francs.

(Hooray! I win another one!)

CHECKING IN...

Ten minutes later, at about 3:15 PM, we arrive at the front entrance to our hotel, the Hotel Castille, (totally unbeknownst to us at the time, the front entrance door of the Castille is located diagonally across the street from the rear revolving doors of the Ritz Hotel.)

Located on the Rue Cambon in the district of the prestigious French high fashion design houses, near the Louvre, the Opéra, and the famous Place Vendôme, the Hotel Castille's decor is inspired by French and Venetian styles; it's a magnificent place to stay... much more luxurious than the White House, too!

TIMELINE: SAT AUG 30 3:15 P.M. ARRIVAL AT BOURGET AIRFIELD, PARIS

"Dodi and Diana arrive aboard Fayed's private jet. They come from Olbia, near the posh resort coast of northern Sardinia, where they have been vacationing on the Fayed family yacht." (USA TODAY, Friday, September 05, 1997, p. 8A).

We check in and go upstairs to our suite, unpack a little, and then (when ya gotta, ya gotta) I nap – I understand Brandon takes a nap for a while, too – while Robin finishes the bulk of the unpacking. Yep, you read that right, folks. (Gotta love it... life is good!)

Robin and Brandon, while I am still napping, each take a shower, and when I wake up some ninety minutes later – which, incidentally, is the *total* amount of "Jack's Rule" relaxing time I ever get in Paris – I follow suit. We're a very clean bunch, what can I tell you?

TIMELINE: SAT AUG 30 4:30 P.M. ARRIVAL AT THE RITZ

"They relax in the Imperial Suite, which reportedly costs $2,000 a night. Diana telephones columnist Richard Kay, of London's Daily Mail, one of her closest friends among the press that has covered her during her 18 years in private life. She tells him she was planning to 'radically' change her life by giving up her public role, though she also tells him she wants to open a number of hospices.

"Fayed calls his cousin and says he hopes he and Diana will marry by the end of the year." (USA TODAY, Friday, September 05, 1997, p. 8A).

Before we leave our suite, at about 5:15 PM, I place a call to my dad in New York (where the time is just after 12 Noon EST), and we all wish him a happy birthday. After that, we get dressed up in our Saturday night best, and now we are ready to rock 'n' roll. By this time, it's 5:30 PM., and we have a big night of site seeing planned. (Hey, but really... what happened to "Jack's Rule?" So quickly forgotten!)

TIMELINE: SAT AUG 30 5:30 P.M. PAPARAZZI CAMP OUT IN FRONT OF, AND IN BACK OF, THE RITZ

CLOSED FOR REPAIRS...

We are hungry and ready for dinner, and we decide to eat at our hotel – one of the main reasons Robin had selected the Castille was because of its location and the great reviews for its restaurant: they bill their restaurant as having the best Italian food in Paris! – so we arrive in the lobby and follow the signs. Well, an unfortunate surprise awaits us as we watch workers sawing wood, hammering away like mad, and doing some major construction work. According to the sign, the restaurant is closed for renovation... one weekend only... *this* weekend. We are not going to be eating here tonight, that's for certain. Not happy.

We check with the Concierge about finding another great place to eat, but he tells us that the best eateries in Paris don't open until 7:30 PM on a Saturday night. And now we're starving!

The Concierge suggests that we exit the hotel from the front lobby door and maybe go site seeing first. He suggests we make a right turn after exiting the front door, in order to start walking in the direction of the heart of the city. Then, as we walk, he says, perhaps we will find, at best, a small bakery or open food shop. "Look for the

Obelisk, walk towards the Louvre."

FORESHADOW...

Well, we leave the Hotel Castille at about 5:45 PM. Unsure of exactly where we're heading, Robin and I do indeed start walking to the right, but then Robin stops in her tracks, turns towards me, and points to the left. Looking diagonally across the street from where we stand, she says, "Jack, look... what do you think's going on over there?"

A hundred feet away or so, in plain view, are a bunch of parked motorcycles, and standing and sitting astride them are some guys with huge camera equipment strapped over their shoulders. Their eyes are focused on one spot near a hotel exit or entrance (I can't tell which), but I have no clue as to exactly what they're up to.

At the time, we have no idea that the Hotel Castille is just steps away from those infamous revolving doors located at the rear entrance to the Ritz. And that's exactly where these people are hanging out. Now I'm curious, and as I take out my camera I say to Brandon and Robin, "Hey, let's check it out!" As Brandon and I start to walk across the street in that direction, Robin will have none of it. She says, "C'mon, you guys, stop wasting time here and let's get into the city already!" (She's definitely back to "Robin's Rule.") Robin is not one to be denied... and so we follow Robin away from that unusual scene, and walk towards the main part of the city.

TIMELINE: SAT AUG 30 6:00 P.M. DODI AND DIANA LEAVE THE RITZ

"Henri Paul returns home believing his day is done. The French magazine VOICI (No. 514, September 15, 1997, p. 14) reports that Dodi and Diana left the Ritz at 18 h 00 (6:00 p.m.), but USA Today says they left at 7:00 p.m.

"At 7 p.m., the two go out the back door of the Ritz and head back to Fayed's apartment. They plan to go out to dinner, perhaps to Benoit, a long established bistro off the Rue de Rivoli (whose manager denies the pair were expected). With the couple gone from the Ritz for the evening, Paul leaves." (USA TODAY, Friday, September 05, 1997, p. 8A).

IS IT SOUP YET?...

The weather outside is gorgeous: clear as a bell, mid-70s, and zero humidity. In a couple of hours, an absolutely perfect summer day is going to be coming to a close.

It's now 6:15 PM as we walk down the Rue Cambon and find a little informal restaurant, where we have some sandwiches for dinner. Feeling invigorated from our light meal, and feeling very well-rested, at about 7:30 PM we decide it's finally time to site see.

TRIP THE LIGHTS FANTASTIC...

So we start to walk in earnest, and the very first sites we see I will never forget: the Egyptian Obelisk in the center square, and as we look to the west we see the Eiffel Tower, and in the south we see the Arc de Triomphe. It is really magnificent... the sites are screaming at us: they say, "*Bienvenue*! You are actually in Paris!"

We begin walking on the Champs Elysees toward the Arc, and we stroll for what must be forty-five minutes or so.

TIMELINE: SAT AUG 30 8:00 P.M. THE COUPLE TRY TO SHOP ON THE CHAMPS-ELYSEES

"At about 8 p.m., the two are driven by Dodi's driver a short distance to Sephero, a large perfume shop on the tourist-choked Champs Elysees. But photographers swarm the car like highwaymen around a stagecoach. Diana and Fayed don't even get out of the car. Instead, the two change for dinner back at the apartment." (USA TODAY, Friday, September 05, 1997, p. 8A).

Twilight is starting to fall, so we decide to buy some tickets for the underground, and we tube the rest of the way to the Arc. As we re-enter street level, Robin leaves us for a few minutes to use a WC, and Brandon and I sit on the curb and wait on the avenue in front of the Arc.

TIMELINE: SAT AUG 30 8:30 P.M. THEY RETURN TO DODI'S APARTMENT

While we wait, we're approached three separate times by little beggar children: first a little girl, then two little girls, then a little boy, all of whom, in turn, ask us for money. We give them some francs and the pretzels we've been eating, which really makes their faces light up. These kids are hungry.

A FATEFUL MEETING...

Robin rejoins us and we climb the hundreds of stairs to the top of the Arc. At its apex we're rewarded with an incredible 360-degree view of the beautiful city of Paris at night. (Fortunately, I *did* remember to bring the binoculars with us.) The most striking site of all is our view of the Eiffel Tower, all lit up and beckoning. I notice an electric sign on it, in which a message glows – L'anni 2000: 854 – and I don't speak or understand French but I do finally figure out that this is the countdown indicating the number of days remaining until the year 2000.

Still atop the Arc, we meet other tourists, a husband and wife – Americans who are stationed in Germany – and Robin learns from the wife that the Seine River cruise is an especially great thing to do at night. Robin learns from her new acquaintance that the ferry disembarks at the plaza across the street from the Eiffel Tower. That's all Robin needs to hear! We soon descend the Arc and take another tube, and then, at about 9:45 PM, we walk the remaining five blocks to the Eiffel Tower.

TIMELINE: SAT AUG 30 9:45 P.M. THE PRINCESS AND DODI DECIDE TO RETURN TO THE RITZ

They leave Dodi's house on the rue Arsene-Houssaye. "Diana is wearing white pants, a black bodysuit, black jacket and sandals. They head back to the controlled surroundings of the Ritz, arriving about 10 p.m., unexpectedly and with 30 photographers on their heels."

(USA TODAY, Friday, September 05, 1997, p. 8A).

We arrive at the Eiffel Tower at about 10:00 PM. From a distance, we take a number of photos of the Tower because we are so impressed with its enormity and simplicity and complexity of architectural design. When we reach the Tower itself, we just stare straight up in awe.

We then cross the street and walk onto the plaza, adjacent to the River Seine. It's a very busy and bustling setting, what with a strip of vendors who sell crepes, sandwiches, assorted ice creams, and bottles of soda and water. There are also a few couples dancing the polka to the rhythm of a live four piece band.

SOLD OUT...

We spot the cruise line ticket office, and I walk up to the woman in the ticket booth to purchase three tickets. Brandon notices a ferry boat docked at port some twenty feet from where we stand, and it's filling up with passengers. The next cruise is getting ready to depart, and I figure our timing is most excellent and that we can board immediately.

But the Frenchwoman ticket seller is giving me a bit of a difficult time – could this be Nasty French Incident # 3? – her accent is thick and I'm just not sure of exactly how much the cost of the cruise is. She barely speaks any English, but she points to a sign indicating the prices... and I whip out my trusty currency converter.

So, after what I'm rather certain are French expletives being hurled my way – and by the time I figure out if she gives me the correct change and she hands over the tickets to me – the cruise disembarks *sans* the Firestones. (I do believe she timed it "just... so.")

The next cruise, we learn, isn't departing for another forty-five minutes to an hour. We have to kill some time... Brandon is hungry and starting to get a little cold and tired, so we buy him a delicious chocolate crepe, cooked up for him by a sweet French lady vendor. At my urging, Robin and I try our hand at dancing a polka for a few minutes, much to Brandon's amusement. And after that, I suggest to

Robin, because the wait is becoming tedious, and because Brandon is now getting grumpy, and is, in fact, *really* cold and tired now (as am *moi*), that perhaps I should see if we can just get our money back, and that we will return for the cruise the following night.

But Robin is not to be dissuaded, and we all stay and wait for the next departure, which isn't until about 11:15 PM. Finally our boat comes in, and we cruise the River Seine for about an hour. It is truly beautiful, and scenic, and full of history... however, one minor complaint: I believe we must be the only Americans on board, because the ship's tour guide speaks over a loudspeaker in both French and English... but the English is very diffident... which could be one of the reasons Brandon falls asleep.

Anyway, we ultimately arrive back on shore at about 12:15 AM. And it's now early Sunday morning, August 31st, 1997. The electric sign has changed slightly; it now glows with the message L'anni 2000: 853. The countdown continues.

CALM BEFORE THE STORM...

TIMELINE: SUN AUG 31 12:20 A.M. DEPARTURE FROM RITZ

"The photographers are waiting. Diana immediately covers her face. A minute later, the casually dressed Fayed comes out of the same door.

"Rees-Jones escorts Diana to the car. She sits on the rear passenger side. Fayed joins her on the rear driver's side.

"Paul has the engine running. Some say he was giddy with the photographers. Others claim he openly boasted, 'Tonight you won't catch us.'

" 'He was laughing a lot. Many said he wasn't his usual self,' says Jacques Langevin of the Sygma agency, one of the photographers under investigation for involuntary manslaughter." (USA TODAY, Friday, September 05, 1997, p. 9A).

"In an interview, [photographer Jacques Langevin] recalled seeing Paul, who police say was drunk, emerge from the Ritz after a decoy van drove off.

"When Diana emerged from the hotel, Langevin said he took four or five pictures before she got into a black Mercedes.

" 'The car took off very fast. My car was up the road. There was no way mine could keep up, so I knew it was finished for me,' Langevin said." (USA TODAY, from wire reports, Thursday, September 04, 1997, p. 2A).

" . . . And the Times of London reports today that the driver had taunted photographers by saying, 'Catch me if you can,' before speeding away from the Ritz hotel where Diana and her friend, Dodi Fayed, had dined." (Fred Coleman and Jack Kelley, USA TODAY, Tuesday, September 02, 1997, p. 1A).

"Des photographes reperent, rue Cambon, la Mercedes 280 S, qui demarre a 0 h 20 avec ses quatre occupants. Les paparazzi la prenent en chasse, rejoints par des confreres, prevenus par portable. En tout, ils sont une douzaine a suivre la limousine noire. A moto and en voiture." ["Some photographers spotted, on the rue Cambon, the Mercedes 280 S, which left at 12:20 with its four occupants. The paparazzi gave chase, rejoined by cohorts called on the portable. In the end, there were a dozen following the black limousine. By motorcycle and by car."] (Internet – Non-vetted source, September 1997)

TIMELINE: SUN AUG 31 12:22 SPEEDING TOWARD THE TUNNEL OF DEATH

LANGUAGE BARRIER...

On the side of the avenue there are several parked taxicabs with their headlights on, ready to do business. Robin walks up to a cab and tells the driver we require a taxi to take us to our hotel, but the driver tells us we need a "réservation" and he indicates a dispatcher. We approach the dispatcher and inform him that we need a car. He directs us to yet another taxicab.

(I cannot help but wonder... is it that some French countrymen just like to make it difficult for Americans? Because, if so, they're doing one helluva fine job.) In broken English the driver impatiently asks, "Where? What street?" and I tell him we don't remember the name of the street. Actually, we don't even remember the name of the hotel... all Robin remembers is that it's located next to the House of Dior... or is it Chanel...? she just isn't certain, either. The driver makes zany hand motions, as if to say he does not want to take us. (I have since learned, "don't fight the tape," but that's another story for another day.)

TIMELINE: SUN AUG 31 12:23 to 12:25 A.M. THE CRASH

"The six-inch-thick dossier compiled by the Prefecture of Police in Paris is labeled simply 'Accident Mortel de la Circulation Date 31/8/97 Heure 00 h 30' . . .

"The file begins at 12:23 a.m., in the Place de l'Alma Tunnel . . ." (Rod Nordland, NEWSWEEK, October 20, 1997, p. 34).

But my Robin is not to be denied: she keeps pitching, and then she happens upon a magic word he does understand... "we're near the *Obelisk.*"

He then, begrudgingly, permits us entry into his taxi. Wow, what a process! The three of us get into the back seat of the cab, with me sitting behind the driver on the left, Brandon in the middle, and Robin on the right. It's now about 12:25 AM.

TIMELINE: SUN AUG 31 12:28 A.M. THE POLICE ARRIVE

"Hailed by passersby while patrolling in the area, the first two police officers reached the scene within five minutes of the accident. In their official report, the officers described the scene thus: 'Numerous people, mainly photographers, were shooting pictures of the right rear of the car, whose door was open.' One of the officers rushed up and attempted to push back the photographers, who offered resistance. They were virulent, pushy and continued to take photos, intentionally preventing him from bringing aid to the victims. One of them pushed [the officer] back and declared, 'You piss me off. Let me do my work. At Sarajevo at least the cops let us work.' " (TIME, October 13, 1997, p. 56). "Vous navez qu'a vous faire tirer dessus et vous verrez." ["You've got no way to coverup and you know it."]

(L'EXPRESS, September 11, 1997)

GO, SPEED RACER, GO!...

We are all tucked into the rear of the taxi as the cab driver starts the engine. He lights a thin cigar and proceeds eastbound.

The cab starts to get smoky and we roll down our windows, but Robin has asthma and starts to choke, and Brandon and I (being a former smoker) hate the smell, so I ask him if he can please get rid of his stogie. So, while he mutters French curses under his breath – this is *definitely* Nasty French Incident # 4 – the driver, with exaggerated embellishment, makes a show out of throwing his thin cigar out the window.

This is exactly the impetus he needs in order to justify his being annoyed at these demanding damn Americans: he is one angry Frenchman! Perhaps this rage of his is the main reason he begins to pick up speed, as he is now driving way too fast on the sparsely trafficked avenue. (He may as well have muttered, in French – and perhaps he did – "Well! I shall show *zem* who is zee boss!").

The three of us in the back seat exchange wide-eyed looks a few times, and we now plead for him to "please slow down!" Either because he doesn't understand English, or, more likely, because he has his mind made up to just speed for the hell of it – NFI # 5? Definitely! – he ignores our repeated requests and continues to drive even faster now, much faster than we think is anywhere near being safe. Robin, Brandon and I are certain that if he continues driving like a madman at this tremendous speed, we will end up in a serious collision.

Thankfully, as the taxi approaches one of the many tunnels we drive through on the way back to our hotel, the driver notices that, up ahead, inside the next tunnel, there is some major traffic congestion starting to form. He is forced to slow the cab down, and he slams the brakes.

Up ahead, I notice some flashing, pulsing blue emergency lights in the distance, inside the tunnel, reflecting off the inside tunnel walls. I suppose our driver sees that, too, because, just as another car blocks our egress to the right to pass us, our driver tries to bear to *his* right and take an exit – I presume it leads to an overpass – in order to avoid becoming a part of the traffic jam straight ahead, which is now beginning to build up inside the quickly approaching tunnel. But our driver is still travelling way too fast and he gets cut off by yet another car on his right which does *not* take the exit, and so now our taxi has but one option: we are forced to go directly *into* the tunnel – I later found out this is called the Alma tunnel – which lay directly in front of us.

Our driver (of whom I now start to think of as "Krazy Kabbie") has to immediately pump his brakes in order to avoid a collision with the cars ahead of his, and there we are, approaching the entrance to the tunnel, with Krazy Kabbie all pissed off, now hitting his head with the open palm of his right hand (I kid you not!), muttering more curses in French (like a lunatic, I swear!), and our taxi becomes part of the stop-and-go bumper-to-bumper traffic which slowly creeps past the blue flashing lights reflected on the tunnel's inner wall.

THE TUNNEL VISION...

There are about a dozen cars ahead of us, and our taxi travels perhaps two miles per hour maximum, at any given point. As we make progress and move forward through the tunnel I can glimpse the actual emergency lights up ahead, near the tunnel's exit. We can also begin to see, well before those emergency lights, and also on our left, the cause of the traffic congestion itself: a rather sizable black car has seriously collided into the opposite wall of the tunnel. It is a crash of major proportions.

Initially, I assume that it must be some kind of accident, but the more I see the less certain I become that "accident" is the right word... some of the things we observe are disturbing, to say the least, so I'm just not sure at this point exactly what to make of it.

TIMELINE: SUN AUG 31 12:29 A.M. THE FIRESTONES OF NEW YORK ARRIVE

"American tourists Jack and Robin Firestone told the Agence France-

Presse news agency that they were in a taxi heading the opposite direction as the Mercedes and saw the wrecked car in the tunnel almost immediately after the accident. Robin Firestone said about five photographers were taking pictures as police tried to remove them from the scene.

"Note: The discrepancy in number of photographers. Dr. Mailliez has just said (above) that there were 10 to 15 photographers when he arrived, and he arrived before the police, yet when the Firestones see police trying to remove the photographers, Robin estimates there are 'about five.' This suggests five to 10 people left the scene when police arrived." (SEATTLE TIMES, Tuesday, September 02, 1997, p. A7).

"Robin Firestone of Hewlett Harbor, L.I., who was visiting Paris, said one of the paparazzi put his camera on the wrecked car's windshield and snapped away.

"Her husband, Jack Firestone, said, 'These photographers were all over the car like sharks after raw meat.' " (NEW YORK POST, Tuesday, September 02, 1997).

Brandon comments that the black car is smashed like an accordion. Frankly, I have never seen such damage done to an automobile in my life... it's barely even recognizable as a car.

As we continue to approach the wreckage, I notice unusual goings-on about the scene to which I've just alluded.

A couple hundred feet up ahead, in the opposite westbound lanes — the lanes in which the crash occurred — I notice a police car which blocks off oncoming traffic from those westbound lanes, preventing additional traffic into the tunnel. In fact, I don't recall seeing any cars enter from that direction, so I find it curious that the police should be on the scene so quickly.

Closer to the crash site (over a dozen years have passed and I can no longer refer to it as an "accident" site) than the aforementioned police car, and also in the westbound lanes, are two policemen who stand next to each other, complacently talking and just observing the frenzy of photographers surrounding the crash... almost as if they're in a theatre watching a movie... and they are completely uninvolved, as if they're obeying orders, perhaps? Hmmm... In the center of the tunnel, where the cement support pillars stand, I see, parked very neatly in a line – located in between two of these pillars – about a half-dozen motorcycles; the cycles are located in between the wreckage and the policemen.

Surrounding the carnage are the just-mentioned photographers, who are working very quickly, methodically and businesslike... snapping photos as rapidly as they can. There is non-stop activity from them as their camera bulbs flash in a cacophony of flickering white light.

Specifically, what they're doing is taking pictures of the interior of the wrecked automobile, from every conceivable angle possible, holding their cameras up to where the windows and windshield would have been, and clicking away like mad. Occasionally, one or two of the photographers runs to another vantage point around the smashed car and then continues to take photos of the interior.

As the entire scene unfolds (for the brief time I see it), it is nothing short of surreal; I can only try, there on the spot, to make it make sense. I don't fathom the thought that these people are paparazzi; rather, I suggest to Robin and Brandon that perhaps the photographers are from some Forensics Department of the French police, and they're taking pictures of the grisly aftermath of a horrific accident as part of a report. "Maybe that's how they do it in France," I surmise. Robin challenges me on this and asks me why they would be working at such a frenetic pace, *running* around the crashed car and almost pushing each other out of the way. I have absolutely no reply to offer her.

Another thought I have is in regard to the crash itself. For some reason I make an assumption that the smashed black car had originally been traveling in the same eastbound direction as we were, and that it must have been going so fast when it hit one of the support pillars that its left front bumper somehow fishtails and goes in between two of the cement pillars. In other words, I speculate, maybe the black car did a 150 degree turn and then smashed into the opposite wall: I consider this as a possibility because the smashed-up car is canted at such an angle that I can't imagine it having gotten in its present position by any other means.

Incidentally, I don't recollect seeing any smoke or steam from the wreckage... just a mass of mutilated metal and glass.

In all, from the moment we first enter the mouth of the tunnel to the moment when we exit, I believe about two to three minutes elapse. The first ninety seconds or so we spend in stop-and-go traffic as we approach the wreckage, but when we are directly across from the crash site, something very bizarre occurs: Krazie Kabbie literally brings the taxi to a dead halt and gives rubbernecking a whole new meaning. It's very strange what he does because, when the taxi is "parked" in the Tunnel, he sticks his neck and upper torso out of his window... and then cranes his neck backwards in an even more exaggerated fashion; his objective, obviously, is to get the best vantage point in order to view the carnage that we're all looking at.

During this transitory interval I focus mainly on two things: the photographers' activity and the policemen's inactivity. It's puzzling, though, as to why such a dichotomy exists at this scene.

(When I think back on it, I realize that the photographers had a rabid zeal for photographing the interior of that car, as quickly as possible, as if they *knew* they had just struck "gold," while the policemen were either totally inept, or they were completely ignorant as to the importance of *who* laid inside the wreckage, or they were following strict orders not to intercede. In any case, how could the police just let the paparazzi take complete control and have a field day?)

To my mind, it has to be a planned happening: (a) the police arrive on the scene so quickly after the crash, and are in position to block traffic, and (b) all of the motorcycles are parked neatly in an organized row. This adds greatly to the "something's rotten here" feel of the entire scenario.

As we spend our last few moments looking at the wreckage, Robin turns to me and says, "Oh my God, I see a woman's body slumped in the front of the car, where the top of the dashboard would be... the blonde... she must have been the driver; it looks like she must be dead." Brandon and I say, "Where?" and Robin says, "Jack, look, oh my God." As I look at the crash I reach for my camera and say, "Should I take some pictures?" and Robin answers "No! What are you even thinking?"

Now our taxi starts to pick up speed and we begin to exit the tunnel. To reiterate, I do not see the woman of whom Robin speaks, as I am focusing elsewhere; there is so much going on at the crash site and there is only so much that any individual can mentally process.

We arrive back at our hotel about 12:55 AM, and by 1:15 AM we are all in bed, ready to go to sleep for the night. As we lay in the dark, Robin tells me she cannot get the mental picture of the woman with the blonde hair, and slightly turned head, out of her mind. Robin faces me and says that she's having trouble getting to sleep... something about the images of the wreckage and the photographers are haunting her. I know just what she's talking about... I am still envisioning the flash bulbs going off a mile a minute. I agree with her that it was an absolutely awful scene, but that we should try and forget it for now, and go to sleep. And soon, thankfully, we do just that.

TIMELINE: SUN AUG 31 4:15 A.M. Princess Diana pronounced dead. (TIME, October 13, 1997, p. 56)

A LATE BREAKFAST...

The next morning we wake up at about 9:45 AM, very late for us. We've become accustomed to waking up almost every day this past week at about 6:15 AM... for Robin's magical site seeing tour! Today we deserve a reprieve.

We're hungry, we brush up and shower, and get dressed... and then the three of us go downstairs to the breakfast room in the hotel at about 10:30 AM. Even though the dinner restaurant from the night before is closed, there is a separate dining area where the staff serves breakfast to the guests.

It feels a bit peculiar during our meal because it is so eerily quiet... in the partially filled dining room it seems as if we're the only English-speaking people... but we don't really think much of it. (The only sounds we hear are occasional French murmurs of whispered conversation, and the sounds of cutlery meeting fine china.)

Anyway, we eat leisurely, discuss our plans for the day (which include going to three different museums), all the while being completely and blissfully ignorant of the hand that fate dealt us.

When we finish eating at about 11:15 AM, Brandon and I go upstairs to our suite to wash up and get ready for the day. The hotel had previously arranged to provide us with museum passes, and Robin says she needs to stop at the Concierge desk first to pickup those passes. She also wants to arrange for an English-speaking driver: no more French taxicab drivers for us, not after last night!

We go our separate ways.

THE TRAGEDY REVEALED...

Brandon and I make our way upstairs to the suite. Our stomachs are full from a delicious breakfast; Brandon flops down at the foot of his bed and, as kids do, he automatically turns on the television set in his room. MTV. I'm in the bathroom brushing my teeth, and when I finish, I walk into Brandon's room, lay down at the head of the bed, and lean against the headboard. I say, "Hey, Bran, let's say we put on some news and see what's happening in the world, shall we?" He says "okay" and I take the remote and change the channel to the BBC or CNN.

On the screen is a woman who is identified as being an AIDS activist, talking about how wonderful Princess Diana *was*, and discussing Diana's accomplishments and involvement with the AIDS crises throughout the years.

I turn to Brandon and say, incredulously, "What's all *this* about? Did Princess Diana die from AIDS, and nobody knew about it?" Brandon just looks at me, as totally dumb-founded as I am.

The next shot on the screen blows us away: there is a photo of Diana, with a caption underneath which reads *"Princess Diana, 1961 - 1997."* We look at each other and both of us say, "What!?" The next shot is another photo of Diana which reads *"Princess Diana, Dead in Paris."* This is just too much! And then the next shot is a picture of the car crash we had seen the night before... just *hours* before, actually! And then it clicks in our heads. It is just too inconceivable!

I say, "Oh my God! Brandon, listen, when Mommy comes up here, don't say anything about this as soon as she walks in the door. We have to make sure she's sitting down first." He agrees.

Brandon and I continue to watch the coverage on the TV screen in utter disbelief, our jaws slack, and a few minutes later Robin opens the door and walks into the room. She wears the exact same expression as us, a look of total disbelief on her face. She and I look at each other knowingly, acknowledging that we each knew what had happened last night, *and* the significance of *what* we saw last night... and here it is, playing out in numbing detail on the small screen, in our hotel room, in living color: our own personal *Twilight Zone* episode.

Robin joins us at the TV; we cannot take our eyes off it. Robin tells us how she found out about Diana's death:

When she goes to pick up the museum passes from the Concierge's desk, Robin asks him how we can get a good taxi driver... an English *speaking one, if you please, "...because we had this awful driver last night and we saw this horrific accident inside a tunnel and it could very easily have been us and our driver was driving very, very fast and..." The Concierge looks at Robin solemnly and, quietly, he says, "Madam, did you not hear who was in this car?" And Robin, her knees starting to buckle, begins thinking, "Who could be in that car in the middle of the night, in Paris, someone that this Concierge and I would* both *know?" So she says, "No... what!?" And finally the concierge says, "Lady D! Lady D!" Robin doesn't comprehend why he is saying "Lady D"...and then suddenly it dawns on her, all the pieces fit together, she can't believe it, and her body starts to shake and she gets weaker in the knees... and her heart sinks.*

"Madam, I am so sorry, it was the Princess Diana." In total shock, Robin asks him if Diana is okay. "No, Madam, not okay, no, I am so sorry to say that she is dead." The Concierge sees Robin go pale, and he apologizes for his direct manner and asks her if she requires assistance to go upstairs to our room. She shakes her head, and then excuses herself as she starts to slowly walk to the small elevator.

Ten minutes later we are still watching the TV news coverage. The room's telephone rings. It's the Concierge, and he wants to know if Robin is all right. He is very concerned, and I tell him Robin is very shaken up, but that she'll be fine.

We are all, however, as I just intimated, in a state of utter shock.

LIFE GOES ON…

Finally, about 12:30 PM, after not taking our eyes off the TV for quite awhile, we decide to get out of the room and, needing something to do – and needing some fresh air; it is, after all, another warm, sunny day here in Paris – we do the only thing we know how to do: site see. But we are in such a daze… in such a state of… incredulity! We are in total disbelief. It has to be untrue…

Trying my best to act noncommittal, I say to Robin and Brandon, "Let's go to the museum, let's try to forget about this for now." All we want to do is to block this out of our minds. Total denial, anyone? It sounds good… for the moment.

The weather is clear and hot, and when we arrive at the Louvre, Robin makes a pit stop at the bathroom. She is feeling overwhelmed, nauseous… and then she overhears the chatter. Even in French, she understands that everyone is talking about Princess Diana. Dead!

We subsequently walk from exhibit to exhibit and from museum to museum. We see many of the great artworks, including da Vinci's Mona Lisa, the Venus de Milo, James McNeill Whistler's "Whistler's Mother," and lots of Monet's. Seeing the artwork certainly distracts our minds away from the tragedy, but as we walk around during the day, we remain in shock.

My mind starts to wander: *How can this be? We were in England only yesterday! While we were in Waterloo Station in London, waiting for the EuroStar to depart, I was thumbing through some tabloids and newspapers, perusing pictures of Di and Dodi on his yacht. Diana was England! And now she's dead! We had just spent the last seven days in the U.K. on an incredible vacation and there was nothing but royalty on our minds! We were in England and so was Diana… alive. And now, here we are, waking up to the news that the Princess of*

England is dead... in Paris, yet! Where we are! It makes no sense! And then, realizing that we were there in the Tunnel... last night... earlier today... realizing that we saw the car crash which killed her... is just way too much to bear.

After watching early reports on television, we know we had seen things that are very different from what was being reported on the news. We hear a lot of speculation and conjecture and misinformation being reported; we know we have to do our civic duty and come forward... if only to truthfully tell what we had witnessed, and to help set the record straight.

THERE'S NEVER A COP AROUND WHEN YOU NEED ONE...

So, about 3:00 PM on Sunday, August 31st, we walk up to a policeman who is on duty in front of the Orangey Museum. He speaks very little English – it seems that nobody in Paris speaks any English, or doesn't want to admit it to any Americans if they do – and we try to communicate to him that we saw the immediate aftermath of the crash which killed Diana last night. He says to us, in broken English, that they have enough witnesses, but, if we want to, we can file a report at police headquarters. (Um, did he just say "they have enough witnesses"?). And that is that; he is not interested any further. As he starts to walk away – he can't walk away quickly enough – Robin says to him, "Excuse me... where exactly should we go to file our report?"

He mentions something about going to the "Petit Palais" or the "Grand Palais" and we actually start to walk in one of the directions he points toward... but we realize we have no idea where we're going, we certainly can't find *either* "Palais," he did not give us a specific address (he only pointed), he certainly didn't seem to care... and besides that, it is freakin' hot out, and trying to converse with this man was tiresome... so we start our journey back to our hotel.

En route, we happen to enter one more museum (just to cool off), and then stop at an outdoor cafe for something to eat and drink. Finally, at about 5:00 PM, we return to our hotel, feeling rather beat from the current day's and previous night's events.

UNANSWERED QUESTIONS...

We turn on the television and watch CNN and the BBC, those being the only sources for news in France (if you don't speak French or German, that is.) We watch for what seems like hours, hardly able to take our eyes off the screen, and it is then that we realize what the real issues are, as expressed by the TV commentators: *"Did the photographers – the paparazzi – cause the accident? Were they involved at all? How many of them were there at the scene? Did they try to assist?"* And I know that we have some of the answers.

CNN promotes a 202 area code (Washington, D.C.) phone number for people to call in with their comments and thoughts regarding the Diana tragedy. I'm thinking of calling to talk about what we saw, and about what we know, but I don't. I think that the best choice for us is to notify the police first.

We shower and get dressed for our appointed dinner, and decide that afterwards we will try again to contact the police.

LE VAUDEVILLE...

I say "appointed dinner" because, back in June when Robin had first made these travel plans, our travel agent Sherry (from New York) had booked dinner reservations for us, on this very date, at 8:00 PM, at a restaurant called *Le Vaudeville*. And as fate would have it, we are seated at a table outdoors, with me facing Robin and Brandon... and a long view of the street beyond.

While we're dining, I notice that there are some interesting looking buildings across the street, one to my immediate left and one that is further away, down the street, on the corner, facing me; this particular building has the letters AFP on it, lit up in red. I ask my waiter what the two buildings are; he says that the nearer one to my left is the stock exchange building, and the further building – the one which I am facing during our entire meal – is the news organization called the *Agence France-Presse*. Never heard of it. He explains that the AFP is a news organization, and Robin and I exchange a long look.

During the course of our entire dinner that evening, as I face this AFP building, I can't help but notice that there are a lot of lights turned on inside, and that every so often I had seen people entering and exiting.

AFP...

So after dinner, at about 10:00 PM, we decide what to do next: do we go to the Latin Quarter, as we had originally planned; or do we go to the AFP and see if we can speak with someone about what we witnessed, thereby seeing if they can help us contact the police. I make the decision for us: we walk down the street to the AFP.

We enter the building lobby and encounter two men who sit in the reception area to our left. I proceed to tell them some details about what we saw last night, but they basically speak no English at all. However, one of the men motions for me to wait a moment upon hearing me say "Princess Diana." He climbs the long set of stairs to the next floor, disappears through a door for a couple of minutes, and reemerges with another man who, as it turns out, works in the news division at the AFP. He speaks some broken English as he descends the stairs and joins us in the main lobby.

We relate the bullet points of our story to him, and when we finish, he asks if we will tell him where we are staying. I give him our hotel's address and he thanks us. As we are leaving through the exit door and he is walking back up the stairs, I yell up to him, "Excuse me, can I have *your* business card?" He says, "Of course. Wait here for a minute, I'll be right down with it." We wait for about five minutes, and then he comes down in the elevator with yet *another* gentleman – *his* boss, I suppose (who, unbeknownst to us at the time, is an AFP reporter) – who speaks *perfect* English. We *again* begin to tell our story to him right there in the lobby, and he interrupts at a certain point and asks the three of us if we wouldn't mind coming upstairs with him so he can file the "report." It seems to be more of a demand than a question, so we acquiesce. I say, "Okay, but we really need your help getting in touch with the police." He assures me that this will be his main priority.

We enter their news bureau and sit down on some chairs, and

the AFP reporter asks us some questions about what we saw. His associate types our responses on a keyboard, verbatim.

(Meanwhile, completely unbeknownst to us, our story is now spreading, via teletype and e-mails, all over the world.)

The AFP reporter then picks up the phone and tells us he is going to call the police for us. He speaks into the phone at length, in French, and after about five minutes he hangs up the phone. He takes out a piece of paper and writes a name and phone number on it; he says that I am to call this number – "the police department," he says – at 10:30 AM tomorrow... Monday... and they will most definitely be expecting my call. We thank everybody for their help, and we leave the AFP building.

We hail a taxicab and give him the address of our hotel. The ride takes about ten minutes, and then the cab stops in front of a building which is not our hotel. The driver says something like, "Here we are," but I say, "This is not our hotel, we are staying at the Castille."

He says he was told to drop us off at the rear entrance of the Ritz Hotel... very curious. This entire ordeal continues to play out even more strangely.

He drives the additional hundred feet or so up the street to the Castille. We enter our hotel, walk up the stairs to our suite, put on the news for a few minutes, then shut it off, and then go to bed.

A FALSE LEAD...

The next morning, Monday, September 1st, we awaken late again, at about 9:00 AM. We get showered and dressed and go downstairs for breakfast. At 10:30 AM sharp, now back in our suite, I pick up the phone and dial the number which the AFP newsman gave me last evening. It *is* the police department, but the person I am talking to speaks virtually no English at all and has absolutely no idea what I'm talking about and certainly, he says, no one is expecting my call. Finally, he says perhaps we might want to try back at about 1500 hours (3:00 PM). Then he abruptly hangs up the line.

OASIS...

A moment later a note is put under our door. It's from a reporter's secretary at the CNN Paris Bureau, asking us to please call them as soon as possible. I dial the number right away, and am asked if we can come down to their studio and give them an interview about what we saw. Robin and I discuss the request briefly among ourselves and we decide to do it... it sounds like the perfect way – finally – to get our story to the police. (In hindsight, Robin and I always wondered why we never even thought to contact the American Embassy.) The secretary gives me CNN's address, and we jump into a cab.

At about 11:30 AM, Robin, Brandon and I find ourselves giving a live ten minute interview to correspondent Walter Rodgers on the rooftop of the CNN building.

After we finish the interview, we're introduced to some other CNN staffers, to whom we tell our main concern, it being that we feel it to be extremely important that the police are contacted immediately. I start to think about Krazie Kabbie from two nights ago... *he knows where we're staying*, my mind wanders again, *and if we do not voluntarily come forward and make every effort to be heard, and if he tells the police he knows where other witnesses are staying, might there be a chance that the police could, perhaps, possibly detain us at the airport tomorrow when we're scheduled to depart Paris for New York? We know that Brandon's school term begins on Wednesday, September 3rd, so we need to do whatever it takes now to tell the police what we saw so that we will avoid the possibility of being arrested and/or interrogated and/or in custody.*

One CNN executive, a wonderful, caring guy named Robert Wiener, is very helpful. He calls the police for us (for real, this time, it seems) and tells them about what we have witnessed; Robert is apparently told by his police contact that the police in charge of the Investigation are very interested in hearing what we have to say, but that they cannot state exactly *when* during the day the police will be able to take our deposition. Finally, Robert's police contact tells him that the police will call him back in thirty minutes to schedule an interview for the Firestones, to occur later in the day.

Robert takes this opportunity to say that he'd love for us to do a live interview on the *Larry King Live* show later tonight. We think about it for several minutes, but we aren't quite sure whether we want to or not. It is further explained to us that we would have to be at the CNN Paris studio at 3:00 AM Tuesday morning in order to be on the 9:00 PM (EST) Monday feed shown live in the United States. Robert pitches us a little bit, as he raises the dual issues of our unique perspective combined with the sheer importance of sharing our story "for the record"; we ultimately give in and agree to do it.

I specifically say to Robert, however, that my biggest hang up is that we would commit to do this interview and have to stay up very late to do it (I'm *not* a night person... Robin is, I'm not), and that at the last minute our appearance would be cancelled. He says, "Hey, Jack, you guys are very big news, and the only thing that would cancel your appearance on the show would be if somebody drops the atom bomb on New York City."

Meantime, over an hour passes, and Robert still has not heard back from the police, so he calls them again. It is now about 12:45 PM. The police tell Robert that they do indeed want to talk to us, but that they still cannot commit to a specific time. This is going nowhere fast... and I then tell Robert of one last "appointment" we have to keep.

Sherry the Travel Agent had reserved for us, again well in advance, prior to our coming to Europe, lunch at the famed Jules Verne Room atop the Eiffel Tower; the wait for reservations are made months in advance. We tell Robert that we have 1:30 PM reservations, and that we want to go back to our hotel and do a quick change into nicer clothes. Robert provides us with a driver / bodyguard by the name of Eric to accompany us... for the duration of our entire stay in Paris, as it turns out. Robert also informs us that lunch will be compliments of CNN... and that CNN will make certain that we get the best table with the best view – the CNN table, if you please – in the restaurant.

Eric then drives us back to the Castille – "take your passports with you, just in case," he says – and he waits for us outside our hotel, in the CNN car.

BELLS ARE RINGING...

As we enter our suite we find about two dozen small envelopes which had been pushed under the door – inside each envelope is a message from a news bureau, newspaper, magazine, or television network from somewhere on the planet – asking us to give them interviews, and "...please, would we call them immediately!" Here's a sample of some of those people who leave said messages:

Anne Swardson, Washington Post
Mr. Dahlburg, Los Angeles Times
Mrs. Berber, BBC
Moira Conway, SBS Corporation, Australia
Paul Newman, BBC, London
Boris Weber, Stern TV, Germany
Mr. Gunilla, CNN International
Christopher Laureling, M6 Channel
Charlie Masters, Sunday Times
Louise Webster, BBC
N. Sauveniere, French TV
Mr. Claveau, Radio RTL

We simply cannot believe this! And then our phone starts to ring – after every conversation we hang it up and it immediately rings again – these calls are from reporters from various parts of the world who are requesting interviews with us; to each one, we inform that we've just given a live interview to CNN a couple hours ago. We instruct the Concierge to take messages and to place a "Do Not Disturb" on our phone.

It is definitely getting overwhelming (and a little bit scary, too.) At one point, we get a phone call from someone who says he's a reporter who is currently in our hotel's lobby, and that he wants to meet with us to explain how he can protect us, and that he will advise us on who to talk to and who not to talk to. He sounds very convincing, and Robin, Brandon and I are discussing whether or not we should really trust this total stranger. Wait a minute, what are we thinking? – trust a total stranger? – we are definitely in Major Tizzy Mode.

We call CNN and ask for Robert's opinion on this; Robert says, for safety reasons, we should definitely just stay with Eric at all times. Robert advises us to stay put and not to leave the suite unless accompanied by him, and equally important, we should not speak to anyone other than CNN. We feel very comfortable with CNN's concern for our safety. (Wow, you really have to hand it to the media... in retrospect, I realized they knew exactly how to lock down a story! It is, after all, show *business*.)

Eric arrives at our suite door a couple of minutes later. As we make our way down to the lobby, we pass by the rogue "reporter?" who called us a few minutes earlier. He does not appear happy as we refuse to talk to him, accompanied by Eric, as we are.

JULES VERNE...

Eric drives us directly to the Eiffel Tower, and we take the elevator high up to the Jules Verne Room. Eric says he will pick us up after we finish lunch, and will then drive us back to CNN.

We are still somewhat traumatized at this point, but we feel great about the CNN factor... and why not? If you can't trust CNN, who can you trust? We finally have found an oasis in the desert...

Let's talk about the lunch: it's *incroyable* and *fantastique*... in a word: unbelievable! But I am also very annoyed; during lunch I am paged at least a half dozen times by various segment producers from the *Larry King Live!* show calling me from Washington, D.C. about our scheduled appearance for much later that night. I'm still not feeling 100% about this, as previously explained: I reiterate on one of those phone calls to a segment producer, that the idea of staying up until 3:00 AM, first of all, with the possibility of being bumped at the last minute, does not sit well with me. The producer I'm speaking with on the phone assures me not to worry about that; she says it will never happen; so I reaffirm that we will definitely appear on the show. (Here's a lesson: what you think about, you may bring about. Stay tuned...)

She tells me that CNN will pick us up at our hotel at 2:00 AM sharp.

Meanwhile, lunch is finished and Eric picks us up and drops us off at CNN HQ. We enter Robert's office to see what kind of progress he is making in our appointment with the police. He still has not heard from them! With us just back from lunch, he calls them yet again, and once more he is handed the standard line that "the police very much want to take the Firestones' depositions, but we still have not scheduled a firm time." (*Incroyable!*) Robert gets very angry. "Look," he says into the phone, "the Firestones are just trying to do their civic duty as Good Samaritans. They shared with us some critical eyewitness accounts that I am certain you want to hear for your Investigation. But," he continues, "if you cannot accommodate them shortly, I guess we here at CNN will have to do a story to air tonight about the complete ambivalence and incompetence of the French police... so be sure to tune in." He calmly hangs up the phone.

THE LOST DEPOSITION...

An appointment is promptly made and we are summoned to give our deposition to the French police at 6:00 PM tonight.

Eric drives us to the police department at 5:45 PM. He parks the car, and on this lightly rainy and cloudy afternoon we four walk down the street and into the *Brigade Criminelle*; a couple of dozen news reporters, cameramen, and photographers are roped off and stationed directly across the street from the building; they are staked outside the *Brigade*, awaiting word as to the fate of the paparazzi, who are detained on criminal charges in the main building into which we now approach.

We walk towards the front doors of the *Brigade Criminelle* and are immediately stopped by two police guards at the entrance. Eric speaks to them in French as regards our 6:00 PM appointment, and the guards permit us entry. We walk across the expansive main lobby and proceed to climb several flights of stairs. The stairwell is drab and dreary.

At the appointed floor, we are greeted by a policeman who sits in the reception area; he inquires, in French, as to what our business is here. Eric explains, in French, who we are, and the police receptionist asks to see our identification and passports. Robin and I give him our drivers' licenses and passports, Brandon surrenders his passport, and then they ask us to have a seat in the reception area. We are told that the police in charge of the Diana Investigation will be with us in short order.

In the meantime... we all have to use the bathroom facilities, and each of us is escorted, in turn, by a stone-faced policeman... wait a minute, who are the criminals here? This is getting nuttier by the minute.

We three then sit in the darkly lit, wooded reception area; it is a setting straight out of a 1940's crime buster's detective novel, hazy cigarette smoke and all. We learn that we are on the same floor as the paparazzi who are being detained.

We wait semi-patiently for about thirty minutes, and then I inquire as to how much longer the wait will be. I am assured that the police will be with us as soon as they can... "another ten, fifteen minutes or so," I am told.

A half hour later and we are still waiting.

At this point we are starting to get hungry, Brandon is getting tired, and we are feeling all but ignored. I again inquire, and am told that we must continue to wait. The wait, we are told by Eric, is due to the fact that the Interpreter who has been summoned is stuck in traffic, but that he will be there soon. But we are given no assurances as to how much longer our wait will be. The police are very unappreciative and inhospitable, to say the least; at one point, even telling me that if we did not want to wait any longer, we could leave!

Finally, at 7:15 PM, the Interpreter arrives, and we are all led upstairs (with the exception of Eric, who is instructed to wait outside) to the offices of the woman police Commandant and the male Lieutenant (the two policemen in charge of the Princess Diana Investigation... according to them, at least.)

The Interpreter is about sixty years old, swarthy... and he wears an old, ill-fitting suit... and his English is terrible! This is the *Interpreter*? What a joke! He looks like a bad guy character out of a vintage Sidney Sheldon novel. I think, *"This is the man who is going to translate French for me? Oh, man, I am in deep shit!"*

We take our seats in the Commandant's office. The Lieutenant sits at the computer keyboard and turns to me and says something in French. The Interpreter translates and tells me that the Lieutenant is going to take my deposition, and that the Lieutenant will type my responses into the computer terminal. We begin.

The Lieutenant asks me about my vitals, including name, address, date of birth, etc. He then asks me, via the Interpreter, different questions about what I saw the night of the crash. I answer the first few questions, but then he asks me some questions that I do not have the answers to... but Robin does... and I tell him that.

The Commandant and the Lieutenant ask us questions, the Interpreter translates, and either Robin or I answer, depending on which of us have the appropriate information with which to answer the particular question.

At one point, Robin talks about "dark cars" she saw in the Tunnel, and a serious exchange of looks immediately takes place between the Commandant and the Lieutenant. The demeanor in the room changes as both officers stand up simultaneously and ask – demand! – Robin to "s'il vous plait" enter an adjacent office with them, in order to question her alone... leaving me and Brandon with the Interpreter. (Robin tells me later that, as the Commandant and the Lieutenant question her in depth about the dark cars, their English suddenly became pretty darn good.)

About twenty-five minutes later the three of them return to the interrogation office to join me, Brandon and the Interpreter.

The deposition process then continues, and lasts, in total, for about an hour. When we finish, the Interpreter claps his hands twice, after which the Lieutenant presses a button on his keyboard and out of his printer pops a two page, single-spaced deposition, which the Lieutenant presents to me. *Voila!* I look at the deposition, I look at Robin, and I look at it again. This doesn't smell good at all: the deposition is written entirely in French. Of course it is! Was I expecting it to be in English? (Well... *yeah!*)

The Commandant, the Lieutenant and the Interpreter converse in French, and then the Interpreter turns to me, as if everything is perfectly normal, and says, "They would like for you to look at the pages and sign them." I reply, "But I don't understand French, you know that... so I don't know what's written here. How can I sign it?"

The Interpreter poses my question to the two officers, and after more French banter amongst them the Interpreter says to me, "Because I am the official Interpreter, I can look at these pages and read to you what is written there. And then you will know exactly what it says and then you can sign them!" He seems extremely pleased with himself.

Suddenly, I feel as if I were trapped once again in that Sidney Sheldon book, and now the plot thickens... it's about my family being unwittingly involved in a case of international espionage, and that I am about to be framed and thrown into the Bastille for something I didn't do. Really, who knows what is written on those pages? I sure as hell don't.

I answer by saying, "I'm sorry, but that's not good enough. And besides, there are responses typed here which are made by Robin, about things that Robin saw and I didn't see. Even if I *was* to sign it, how could I sign about things that Robin said? Shouldn't *her* responses be in her own deposition?" The Interpreter, the Commandant and the Lieutenant (aka "The Three Stooges") go back and forth on this one, and finally the Interpreter says, "Monsieur Firestone, you said that you and your family were tired of all the waiting, so we made it easier for you by combining all the statements that you and your wife made, and we put it into *one* deposition. So, please... sign it, so we can go!"

I look at the papers again and I say, "Well, the only way I can sign this deposition is if, above my signature, I am able to write 'I cannot read, write, or speak French.'" They are getting pissed off at me now, and the Interpreter says, "But monsieur, if you sign it that way, then we cannot use it." (which part of me thinks is their idea the whole time.) Now the Interpreter and the Commandant converse back and forth in French, and finally, because the hour is getting late, and they clearly have no intention on providing me with a translated copy, they say that it is alright for me to sign it on my terms. And that is precisely how I sign the deposition.

[Note: This deposition "disappeared" for over ten years, only to resurface in October 2007 by Mohamed Al Fayed's legal team; Robin and I subsequently gave live testimony two months later, in London, at the Royal Courts of Justice for the "Coroner's Inquests into the Deaths of Diana, Princess of Wales and Mr. Dodi Al Fayed" on December 3rd, 2007.] But I digress.

As a show of good faith, as we are leaving, the two policemen give Brandon a couple of awesome gifts: an authentic dark blue Paris Police Cap and a Paris Police Badge. Wow! (I never really thought they should be giving gifts to witnesses. Would you think they should? But they do.)

And since the ice is broken, I ask the three of them if they will pose for a photo with Brandon, and I was surprised that they obliged. It is another great photo op. (Man, talk about your Inspector Clousseaus!)

Okay... it's now 8:15 PM, and I know we have a long night ahead of us. As Eric drives us back to our hotel, we stop along the way at a McDonalds, and I run into the joint to pick up a few burgers and bags of fries for our dinner to take back to the hotel. It has been a very arduous day.

NEWS TRAVELS FAST...

Eric parks the CNN car in front of our hotel, and we all get out and enter the lobby. As we walk to the registration desk to ask the Concierge if we have any messages, a lone voice rings out from an adjacent anteroom: "Mr. Firestone? Mrs. Firestone?" We turn in the speaker's direction, and I see, on closer examination, that he is a TV news reporter, because he is flanked by a guy who comes out of the shadows holding a boom microphone, and another guy with a TV camera which points directly at us. The accents of these fellows are most definitely pure BBC.

In addition, also coming from out of nowhere, are a dozen other TV and press reporters from all over the world... the U.K., Germany, France, Italy... all of them aggressively, yet politely, asking for the favor of "exclusive" interviews. We are very tired, but I acquiesce (to Robin's dismay) and grant one interview for all the reporters assembled.

"But first you have to grant *me* something," I say to all those gathered – I'm getting punchy – and at my request they politely pose while I take a group photograph of *them... turnabout is fair play*, I'm thinking... and I am a camera bug, after all, and you never know what I'll want to take pictures of... Good photo ops don't come easy.

THE CURIOUS CASE OF "LARRY KING LIVE!"...

After the interview is finished, it's about 9:30 PM. The three of us go upstairs to try and sleep a little. Brandon dozes off right away, and Robin and I, knowing that we are to be picked up by the *Larry King Live!* people at 2:00 AM sharp, try to rest. But sleep does not come easy; at best, we manage a light snooze.

At 12:00 Midnight, the *Larry King Live!* producer calls our room for a "pre-interview," which we learn is rather common practice on TV talk shows. She conference calls us in with Scott MacLeod of *Time Magazine*, who is also scheduled to appear on our *Larry King Live!* episode.

At 1:00 AM on Tuesday, September 2nd, we get out of bed and take showers, and at 1:30 AM, the phone rings: it's the *Larry King Live!* talent booker. *Here it comes... I can just feel it!* She says that she has bad news for us: they have to cancel the interview, that it has something to do with their being able to "snag" Liddy Dole as a guest [*huh? Liddy (Libby?) Dole? What the hell does Liddy Dole or Libby Dole have to do with anything?*]... so, as a result, they are going to bump our segment.

I am livid! As I suspected... as I *intuited* all day... my self-fulfilling prophecy comes true: in the middle of the night, at the very last minute, they cancel our appearance on the show. I am incensed, even more so because of the very "matter of fact" and indifferent way that we are bumped. I feel jilted: such a big build up and such a fast let down. They are completely oblivious to the great inconvenience this causes me and Robin...

I've since learned that this is exactly what the media does: they chew you up, and then they either swallow you whole or spit you out. We have just experienced both the former and the latter.

Truth be told, though, we are actually relieved that we aren't going to do the show because we are mentally and physically drained.

Before getting ready to go to sleep, knowing that we are leaving in late morning for New York, I check our phone machine at home; we have messages from, amongst many, *Good Morning America* and *The Today Show*, each requesting exclusive interviews when we return to New York.

After listening to those messages, Robin and I look at each other, roll our eyes in disbelief, and then drift off to a deep slumber. Brandon slept through it all. Good for him!

GOING HOME...

We awaken to Tuesday morning, September 2nd, and it is time to be going home! Eric meets us at our hotel and is ready to drive us to the airport. At our request, for a little bit of closure, we explain, we ask him to please first drive us through the now reopened Alma Tunnel. Eric gladly obliges... he drives slowly as our car enters the Tunnel, heading westbound, retracing Diana's, Dodi's, driver Henri Paul's (and Diana's bodyguard Trevor Rees-Jones') last ride in the black Mercedes, driven just three nights ago.

On the roadway surface inside the Tunnel, if you look carefully, I see scattered pieces of the crashed Mercedes in the area nearby the thirteenth pillar.

We arrive at the airport, and with some extra time to pass before we're permitted to board, we stroll over to the duty-free shop in the terminal. After all, there was certainly no time in Paris for Robin to shop (and believe me, that is *always* on her agenda: Robin was born to shop: site see, dine fine... and shop!)

We are immediately recognized by some fellow shoppers who saw us interviewed on TV the night before; a couple of them start to follow us as we walk around the store.

First come the stares, then come the whispers. Finally, people actually come up to us and ask things like "Aren't you the Americans, the witnesses we saw on TV?" "Did you really see her body?" "Was she alive?" "What did she look like?" "Did the photographers cause the accident?" More and more questions. It is certainly overwhelming... especially because we didn't ask for this! People are staring at us now even more, whispering, pointing, and following us at close distances. There is even a couple who asks us for our autograph. The questions, the probing, the stalking and the staring are making us extremely uncomfortable. (And this is the tiniest fraction of what Diana lived with, day after day, as she was chased.) It's as if *we* are famous. How weird. Robin and I are still in awe that this has not gone away. Robin just wants to block it from her mind; we all do... but it is really taking a toll on my wife.

All we really want to do is to go home and forget this ever happened. Somehow I know that will not be the case.

(Am I being too melodramatic?)

As we check in for our return flight, the airline gate attendant recognizes us. She looks at us twice, a double-take of sorts. Robin is exhausted and upset, and the gate attendant asks Robin if everything is okay. Robin says, "No, everything is *not* okay." Robin tells her how people are just staring at her, that she is feeling very uncomfortable, and very nervous. The gate attendant then says "Ummm, just a minute... there are *three* of you traveling today, *oui*?" After we nod our heads, the gate attendant informs us that she will bump us up to First Class.

And at last, after what seems like an eternity, we board the plane.

We settle into our seats, but we're unable to sit next to one another because the flight is so overbooked; we are kind of strewn around the First Class cabin in sporadic seats, but we don't care. We are happy to be seated up front... fewer passengers, fewer stares.

The stewardess carries an armful of newspapers in a few different languages, and as she walks up and down the aisles, she smiles at the passengers and asks which language newspaper they prefer. Among the many newspapers are *L'Actualite* and The Times. And the front page of each and every paper headlines the horrible tragedy of Princess Diana and Dodi Al Fayed, of course. As a matter of fact, most of the contents of all the newspapers have numerous stories, details, and photographs of this tragedy. And there it is: our names. I first see it in The Times. "American witnesses." Quotes and misquotes... *lots* of misquotes... of what we told the authorities. Then, I look in a few other papers. There it is again, in French and German. I could recognize our name: it's Firestone in any language. I can't believe that our names are in these international papers.

Robin is trying to relax and settle into her oversized leather seat. I am hesitant to tell her about our names being in the papers, but I tell her, anyway; she just looks at me with wide eyes and shakes her head.

Soon, a duty free attendant walks up the aisles, and stares directly at Robin. She approaches Robin and then kneels down, as if to share a confidence. She immediately tells Robin how very sad she feels for what we are in the middle of. And then she starts to interrogate Robin about what we had witnessed.

Robin starts to cry – what else is there left *to* do? – it is just too much for her; she can't handle it anymore.

The duty free attendant sympathizes again. She tells Robin that, if the other passengers bother her, to please let the other flight attendants know. (*You* are bothering her, duty free attendant! Leave her alone already!) With that, Robin bolts to the bathroom, and it must have been a half hour before she returns to her seat, as the captain says to get ready for takeoff. It seems that the entire airline staff is given the heads-up as to who we are.

We really believe, though, that by the time we get home to the States, the whole thing will be done, finished, kaput... that it is just going to blow over. Boy, are we in denial.

When our flight lands at JFK Airport, we are greeted at the door of the plane by a half dozen airport personnel, standing in a row, wearing very official-looking Red Jacket uniforms. As Brandon gets ready to exit the plane, he is asked by one of them, "Are you Brandon Firestone?" and he is asked to "step aside, please, and wait here with us until your parents disembark the plane, please..." He has no idea, nor do we, of what is going on here. Robin is the next to exit. Startled and confused, she really has no idea how they know who we are, and more importantly, why they want us shunted off to the side. Robin wonders if there is some sort of a family emergency at home. Then I come off the plane and join my family.

We are advised that over a dozen members of the media are at the airport and they want to interview us right here, right now, for newspaper and TV newscasts. The media had been scouring the airport for hours, they tell us, thinking we are going to change our scheduled flight home to divert the press. (Divert the press? That was the furthest thing from our minds! Crazy! But it gets worse...)

An airline personnel informs us that they were tipped off by a "source" that our home is, and has been, staked out for the last couple of days with dozens of reporters and satellite trucks, etc., so, in addition to members of our local police force "keeping the peace" in front of our house, there is quite a scene waiting for us there. "A media frenzy," the airline personnel informs us.

Robin starts crying again. We cannot believe this. We are told that it will be in our best interests to meet with the press at the airport – *now* – and that the airline already has a press area sectioned off for the interviews. The manager for the Red Jackets tells us that she has it on good authority that, if the Firestones give the media what they want *now* – that is, a press conference or a brief interview – then the media at our house will disperse shortly thereafter.

After going to the bathroom to splash cold water on our faces, we are escorted to a roped-off area. We're greeted by a huge crowd of reporters, yelling for our attention and putting cameras in front of our faces... very similar to what took place in the Alma Tunnel a few nights ago, there is non-stop activity from the paparazzi as flash bulbs from their cameras continue to strobe in a cacophony of white light.

FAST FORWARD: ONE YEAR LATER...

That's what happened during the first few days following August 31, 1997... I haven't touched on the weeks and months and years that have transpired since then in this journal. One day, when Robin and/or I are ready, we'll do precisely that. But in the meantime...

Who could ever have imagined it? And who would have thought, exactly one year later, nearing the anniversary of Princess Diana's death, that we would once again be landing on the tarmac of the

Charles de Gaulle Airport in Paris... only to be arrested as we're greeted by an ominous contingent of airline officials, detectives, and French police... but we were!

The odds were 6 billion to one. The events we experienced were far too incredible to have actually taken place. But they did take place... perhaps, so, that we could get much more of the whole story out there, without a lot of it being whitewashed. Because, contained in our entire story, are the small truths... read between the lines... and if you're really paying attention, you'll notice how those small truths... reveal the bigger truths.

History *is* stranger than fiction. And history, being very objective, never tells the whole story. And the truth has no agenda.

AFTER-WORD

10 Years Later: 2007

A Final Word...

Friday, November 30, 2007

On our way to JFK Airport, sitting in the back seat of a cab, I turned to Robin and said I felt as though I were in a dream. Here we were, over ten years after witnessing the melee in the Alma Tunnel on August 31, 1997, and we were finally going to get our day in court. In other words, we were finally going to not only get closure, but we would, for the first time, be able to tell our story to people who actually were interested in the minutest details of what we experienced during those few days in Paris.

How often in life does one have the opportunity to be a bystander to history?

All too often, over the years, whenever we were interviewed by the media, they would ask astute questions and be fascinated by our responses, but what would show up on the TV screen, for instance, would be pure insipid pablum. A very recent case in point, a few months ago, had been Greta van Susteren's Fox News Channel show "On The Record." Greta and her team had interviewed us for about four hours asking us intimate details of what we had seen ten years ago... but what showed up on the TV screen during its actual airing were the silly "warm up" questions and answers (e.g. "What did you think of Diana when you were in England?", "What did the public think of Charles and Dodi?", ad nauseum). We couldn't believe that her producers didn't air the incisive stuff... and when I followed up with the producer days later, she blamed it on the fact that there was just So. Much. Firestone. Footage. And they were in a last minute time crunch, and that it was easiest to go with the basic questions for editing purposes.

The same thing happened with an interview we did for CBS Morning News in early August 2007. They wanted a broadcast TV exclusive, which we gave them. We were interviewed for hours; the interviewers (including Sheila MacVicar) were fascinated with what we had revealed... and yet, on the day of the taped telecast, our entire interview lasted for about ten seconds, if that.

It was almost as though, what we had to say, had constantly been quashed because of what we had seen. Well, this was going to be different! Our story would, once and for all, finally be revealed... in its entirety.

Saturday, December 1, 2007

We arrived in London 9:30 AM local time. We were exhausted upon deplaning, and we looked for our driver, which had been prearranged for us by barrister Stuart B. and Harrods Department Store.

We got into the car and travelled to a hotel that the court was paying for. It was located in a rather depressing neighborhood, called the Hotel Mercure. We ordered some room service and slept the day away. We later hopped in a car and went to Covent Gardens and had dinner at a French restaurant (Jardin something...) It wasn't until midway through dinner that we realized we were eating in a French restaurant and that we were staying at a French hotel. In London. Ironic.

Sunday, December 2, 2007

Robin and I spent the day touring Kensington Palace, the home of the late Princess Diana. It was so ironic to us, because ten years earlier, having used a book of coupons we had purchased which granted access to so many tourist sites in and around London, one of the very few sites we did not make time to see, of all places, was Kensington Palace.

After spending several hours touring the Palace, and watching moving video and looking at stills of Diana – as well as touring the quarters of Kings and Queens of yore – Robin and I had tea and crumpets in the Orangery.

That night, we had dinner in our hotel. Still very jet-lagged, we went to bed early.

Monday, December 3, 2007

We ate lunch with Stuart B. at the Hotel Savoy at around 12 Noon. He told us that Mohammed Al Fayed (MAF) wanted to have lunch with us tomorrow.

The purpose of our lunch today was to go over the details of the upcoming Court Inquest that afternoon.

We were scheduled to appear in Court promptly at 1:30 PM, so after lunch, the three of us walked towards the Court. At the entrance, Stuart left us in the capable hands of one Martin Smith, Solicitor for the Court. Martin escorted us down a warren of interior courtyards and narrow lobbies until we arrived at a small chamber, where we were instructed to wait until we were summoned.

At a few minutes before two, Martin reappeared and we followed him down yet another long maze of lobbies until we arrived in the courtroom. We sat in the room's left-most corner, and promptly at 2:00, Lord Justice Scott Baker appeared from behind his judge chair. We all rose, and then we all sat down.

I was the first to be called to the stand. After swearing on the Holy Bible, I gave my testimony, a copy of which is available on the court website. (Note: mine consists of 23 pages of typed testimony; Robin's consisted of just 3 pages. More on this in a moment.)

I was asked very pointed questions by barristers (attorneys) named Mr. Hough (see pages 94, 102-104) and Mr. Keen (see pages 111-112) and although our entire Hearing Transcript is not presented in this book, I believe a few excerpts of mine are very telling, in terms of the lack of thoroughness with which Robin's and my testimony was taken. Witness (no pun intended) the following:

CORONER'S INQUESTS INTO THE DEATHS OF
DIANA, PRINCESS OF WALES AND MR DODI AL FAYED

From the 3 December 2007 – Afternoon session hearings transcripts:

PAGE 94

...A. Well, I know that I am right in terms of what I saw. I know that my wife had seen other things that I had not seen. But as far as what I saw, I saw a police car in the position that I just mentioned a few minutes ago...

PAGE 102

...Q. When the interview [JF NOTE: i.e., the deposition of Sep 1, 1997] did happen, I think it lasted about an hour. Is that right?

A. About an hour, yes.

Q. At one point in the interview, I think the officers took your wife to a separate room and asked her some questions on her own.

A. That is correct...

PAGE 103

...Q. Now, you have had the chance to review that statement [JF NOTE: again, the Sep 1, 1997 deposition] since then and I think that you say that one point in it is factually wrong, which is the point we have already dealt with about the position of the police car.

A. I have a copy of that translation here.

Q. ...having looked at it clearly very carefully yourself, are you aware of anything in it that is factually wrong, other than the account of where the police car was?

A. Yes.

Q. What?

A. A number of items, not the least of which is that there are some statements in here that intimate that they are

PAGE 104

my statements when in fact they were my wife's statements...

PAGE 111

...Q. Just above that in the statement, it says:

> "I recall [meaning you, Jack Firestone] that there was a man who was standing on the central reservation in front of the crashed car and telephoning using a cellular telephone"

Was that statement, attributed to you, factually correct? Did you give that evidence yourself?

A. No.

Q. The immediately preceding paragraph says:

> "I [meaning Jack Firestone] remember that there were two or three vehicles parked, but I cannot describe them."

Now did you say that?

A. No.

Q. Two paragraphs earlier than that, it says:

PAGE 112

> "In answer to a question regarding the persons taking the photos, I think there were about five or six."

Did you say that, that there were five or six photographers?

A. No.

Q. I think you told us that there were about a dozen, in fact, round the vehicle.

A. That is correct.

Q. At the top of the second page of the statement it says, "We also glimpsed the body of a blonde woman collapsed forwards." Did you ever say that you had glimpsed the body of a blonde woman collapsed forwards?

A. No.

Q. How would you describe what you have now seen in this statement in terms of accuracy and reliability?

A. I think it is an abomination....

Afterwards, a debate began as to whether or not Robin was going to be called at all, as the Judge was feeling that everything which I had said was sufficient. There were lawyerly debates on this topic, and it happened that, a few minutes later, Robin was begrudgingly called to the witness stand.

She wasn't given a chance to say too much, however. And after just a few questions, Robin stepped down from the witness box, full of tears.

[Only as a point of curiosity will I mention this weird fellow who was watching the courtroom proceedings, He was wearing, on both sides of his face, Diana's name and Dodi's name, painted in thick blue marker. When Robin and I were about to depart the courtroom during the short break that followed her testimony, he approached me and asked if I would donate to some charity or other, and if I would sign a petition he carried. I told him, "no." It was surreal, like out of "Alice In Wonderland."]

But the fact is that Robin and I were feeling kind of low, Robin the more so, because once again we felt we were stymied in our attempt to get our entire story told... and because of her very few minutes on the stand before being summarily dismissed by Baker:

From the 3 December 2007 – Afternoon session hearings transcripts:

PAGE 133

...LORD JUSTICE SCOTT BAKER: Thank you very much indeed, Mrs. Firestone, that will be all. Thank you.

A. There is something that I would like to say. Am I allowed to say something?

LORD JUSTICE SCOTT BAKER: Well, you can say it, but if it is not on the point, we will not really be very interested.

A. I do believe it is to the point because I wish I was

asked a question that my husband was asked. You know, we are different people. I just want to clarify a couple of things...

PAGE 134

LORD JUSTICE SCOTT BAKER: I have just received a note that the shorthand writers are absolutely desperate for a break because we have got further than we would normally, but I think we have the point –

A. Well, I am not sure if you did. However, if this is the point that it is, I feel once again that here I am, all the way in England, and I know what I saw and I would like to say what I saw, but once again it just seems that where the French said that the investigation is totally 100 per cent complete and Scotland Yard said it is 100 per cent complete, that I am being shunned, and if that is the way that it is, then that is the way that it is and I thank the court, and that is that, I suppose. Thank you.

Robin felt absolutely horrible at not being able to get her day in court. As we were getting ready to leave the courtroom and the court building – neither of us saying a word – Martin Smith asked if we wanted to exit via the rear, in order to avoid the reporters. Robin said to him, "I don't live my life in fear" and we left from the front door. And we were confronted by an onslaught of reporters and journalists and photographers and videographers.

One of MAF's executives from Harrods, a wonderful lady named Susan O., told us that our combined testimony went "perfectly." She particularly called notice of the fact that I had referred to the initial French deposition process from 1997 as an "abomination." She said once I said it, that word was all abuzz in the courtroom spectator arena.

Stuart B. then joined us on the sidewalk and said that, in his opinion, the fact that the judge wouldn't permit Robin to testify more than she did was "brilliant." (That's an oft used word in Great Britain and I love it!) He said, "I wish I could take credit for planning the entire day's events as far as our testimonies went." The fact that Robin was prevented from giving her complete testimony seemed to have worked in MAF's favor, certainly not in the favor of the court.

Susan O. said that MAF, as a token of gratitude, wanted to send us to a better hotel, so he arranged for us to be put up at the upscale Millennium Hotel, in the heart of London (Knightsbridge.) Robin and I spent the evening window shopping and having a nice dinner at a quaint Italian restaurant.

Tuesday, December 4, 2007
We awoke late. I called Stuart B. to see what time we were to meet MAF, and he told us that, unfortunately, MAF had been called out of town to Paris, but that, in addition to buying us lunch today at the beautifully ornate Georgian Room, he very much wanted to meet with us tomorrow for a late lunch / tea before we departed for the airport. We absolutely agreed to be there!

In the meantime, at about 1:00 PM, Robin and I entered Harrods, and we took the lift up to the Fourth Floor, to have lunch. We sought out the Maitre d', and as soon as we told him our names, this fellow was running – not walking fast – but running, to make certain that our reserved table was ready for us.

Robin and I sat down at what was probably the best table in the house, overlooking the lavish Christmas decorations. The restaurant was beautiful! And as soon as we sat down, listening to the live piano player / singer, I said to Robin, "Listen! I can't believe what he's playing!" And sure enough, it was "Candle In The Wind." Listening to that song, in the context of where we were, literally gave us the shivers.

Susan O. joined us at 1:15 PM, followed by Stuart B. at 1:20, and the bottles of champagne overflowed.

Susan informed us that my photo, and a story about Robin and me, appeared in the *Daily Express* and that there was an ongoing TV news report about us on Sky Channel last evening.

Stuart told us that, as regarded yesterday's court action, he had never seen the judge's behavior – or the barristers' behaviors – as "challenging" as was exhibited in front of the Firestones. (I guess Robin and I have that affect on people.)

After the main course, Robin and I lingered over our opulent lunch for the next hour and a half. We spent the remainder of the afternoon shopping in Harrods. We took photos of the Diana and Dodi Memorial and posed in front of it ourselves. We also bought tickets, at Harrods' Ticket Booth, to see the musical "Wicked" that night.

As our new hotel was literally a few hundred feet away from Harrods, we went back to take a nap, then took a cab and saw the show.

Wednesday, December 5, 2007

1:30 PM – time for another lunch in the Georgian Room. We approached the same table we had yesterday, sat down, and was then informed by the Maitre d' that instead, we were to dine at MAF's table. As we were escorted to a private corner table, the waiter said to me – and I have to laugh – "You are very famous in America, no?" I said, kiddingly, "Only a little famous, not very." He said, "Very famous." I said, "Just a little." And the waiter said to Robin, "Madame, would you like a fresh glass for your champagne?"

At 2:30, Mohammed and Susan O. approached our table, bearing gifts. MAF gave me two great looking Harrods ties (one red, one green, 'tis the season) and a twelve-year-old bottle of Harrods' scotch. Robin received a beautiful silk scarf and perfume. We hung out and chatted with MAF for about an hour… and Robin finally got the chance to do what she had intended to do in 1997 when she wanted to leave that message for him at the Ritz Hotel: to offer her most sincere and heartfelt condolences to Mr. Al Fayed on the loss of his son Dodi ten years earlier… and to talk with him about the very fragility of life itself.

As the princes have recently stated, one never really gets over the loss of a family member whom we hold dear.

Jack Firestone
May 4, 2017

Jack Firestone, Mohammed Al Fayed, Robin Firestone (December 5, 2007)
The Georgian Room at Harrods of London

CORONER'S INQUESTS INTO THE DEATHS OF
DIANA, PRINCESS OF WALES AND MR DODI AL FAYED

Mr & Mrs Firestone
1 Payne Circle
Hewlett
New York 11557

10 December 2007

Dear Mr & Mrs Firestone

EVIDENCE

I am writing on behalf of the Coroner, Lord Justice Scott Baker, to thank you for giving evidence on 3 December 2007

The Coroner is very grateful for your help. He understands that giving evidence, particularly in relation to the events that took place there 10 years, may cause inconvenience to those involved. However, it is invaluable for the jury who will reach verdicts in relation to how these deaths occurred to hear the oral testimonies of various witnesses and this is the reason he asked you to testify.

Thanks again for your help

Yours sincerely,

Martin Smith
Solicitor to the Inquests

Royal Courts of Justice, Strand, London, WC2A 2LL
Tel +44 (0) 20 7073 1655 **Fax** +44 (0) 20 7947 7112 **Email** admin@scottbaker-inquests.gsi.gov.uk
Website www.scottbaker-inquests.gov.uk

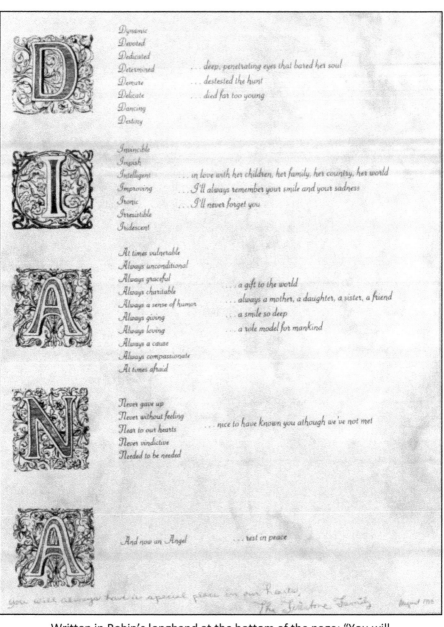

D
Dynamic
Devoted
Dedicated
Determined   . . . deep, penetrating eyes that bared her soul
Demure   . . . destested the hunt
Delicate   . . . died far too young
Dancing
Destiny

I
Invincible
Impish
Intelligent   . . . in love with her children, her family, her country, her world
Improving   . . . I'll always remember your smile and your sadness
Ironic   . . . I'll never forget you
Irresistible
Iridescent

A
At times vulnerable
Always unconditional
Always graceful   . . . a gift to the world
Always charitable   . . . always a mother, a daughter, a sister, a friend
Always a sense of humor   . . . a smile so deep
Always giving   . . . a role model for mankind
Always loving
Always a cause
Always compassionate
At times afraid

N
Never gave up
Never without feeling
Near to our hearts   . . . nice to have known you although we've not met
Never vindictive
Needed to be needed

A
And now an Angel   . . . rest in peace

you will always have a special place in our hearts.
The Firestone Family   *August 1998*

Written in Robin's longhand at the bottom of the page: "You will
always have a special place in our hearts. The Firestone Family"

Created by Robin Firestone, this parchment, dedicated to the
memory of Princess Diana, was placed by Robin & Jack at the Diana
One Year Memorial in Paris (August 31, 1998)

CPSIA information can be obtained
at www.ICGtesting.com
Printed in the USA
LVHW041624151019
634269LV00009B/495/P